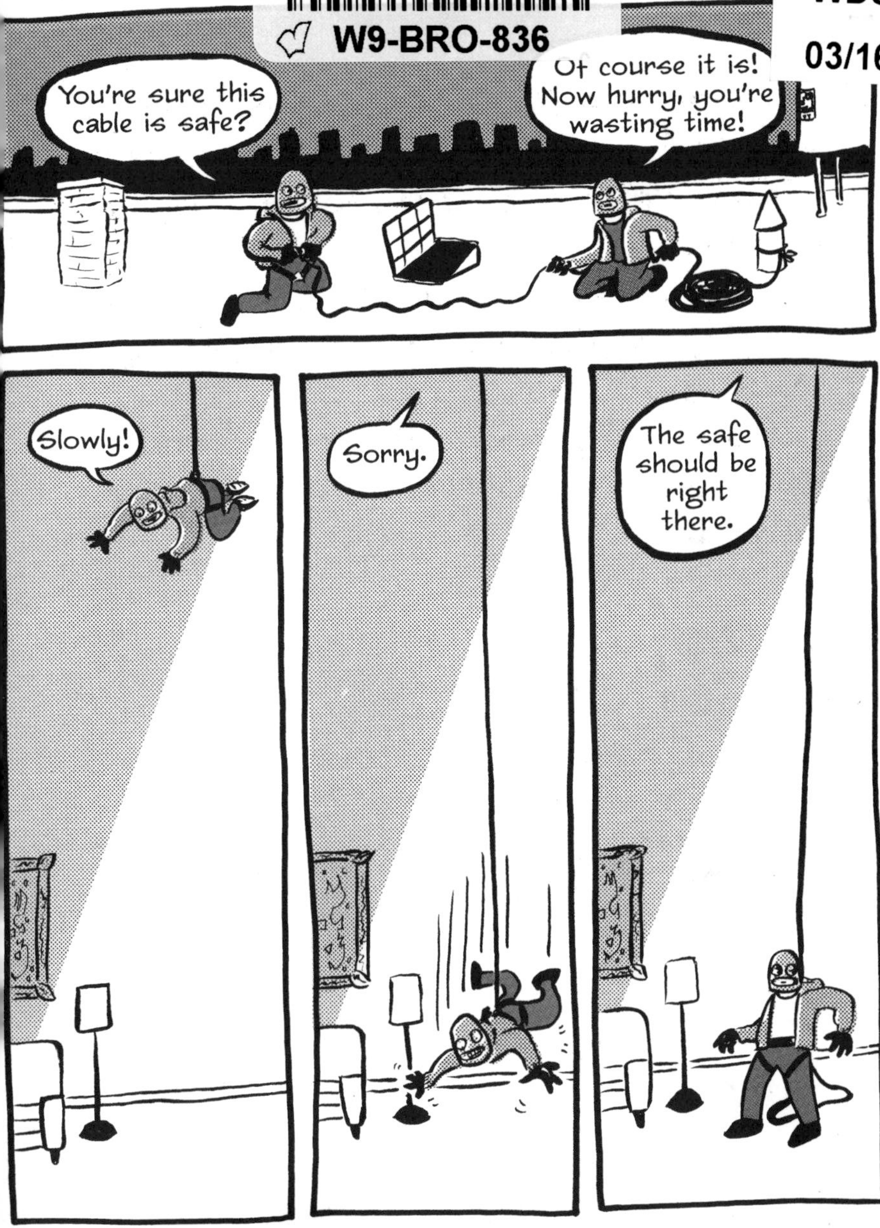
You're sure this cable is safe?
Of course it is! Now hurry, you're wasting time!
Slowly!
Sorry.
The safe should be right there.

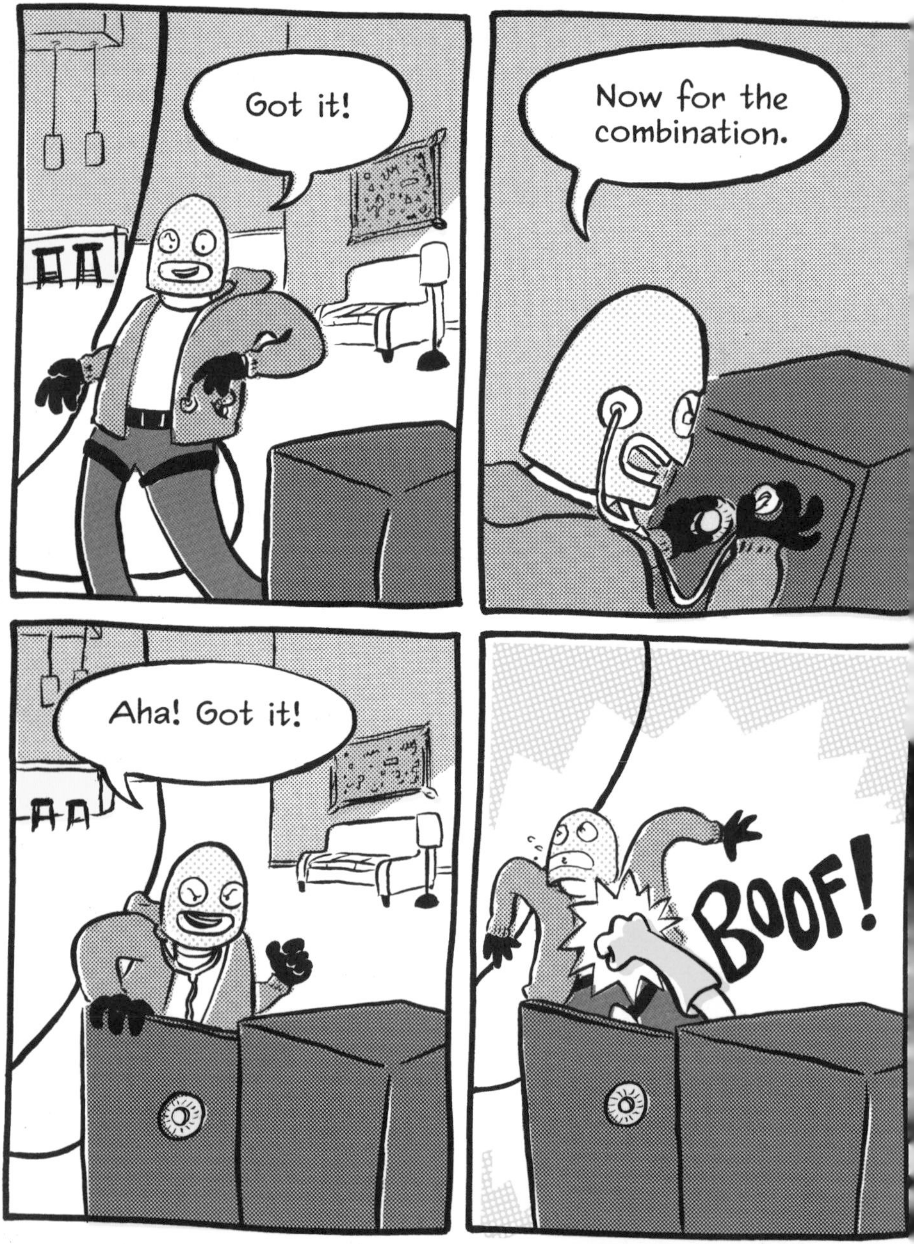
Got it!
Now for the combination.
Aha! Got it!
BOOF!

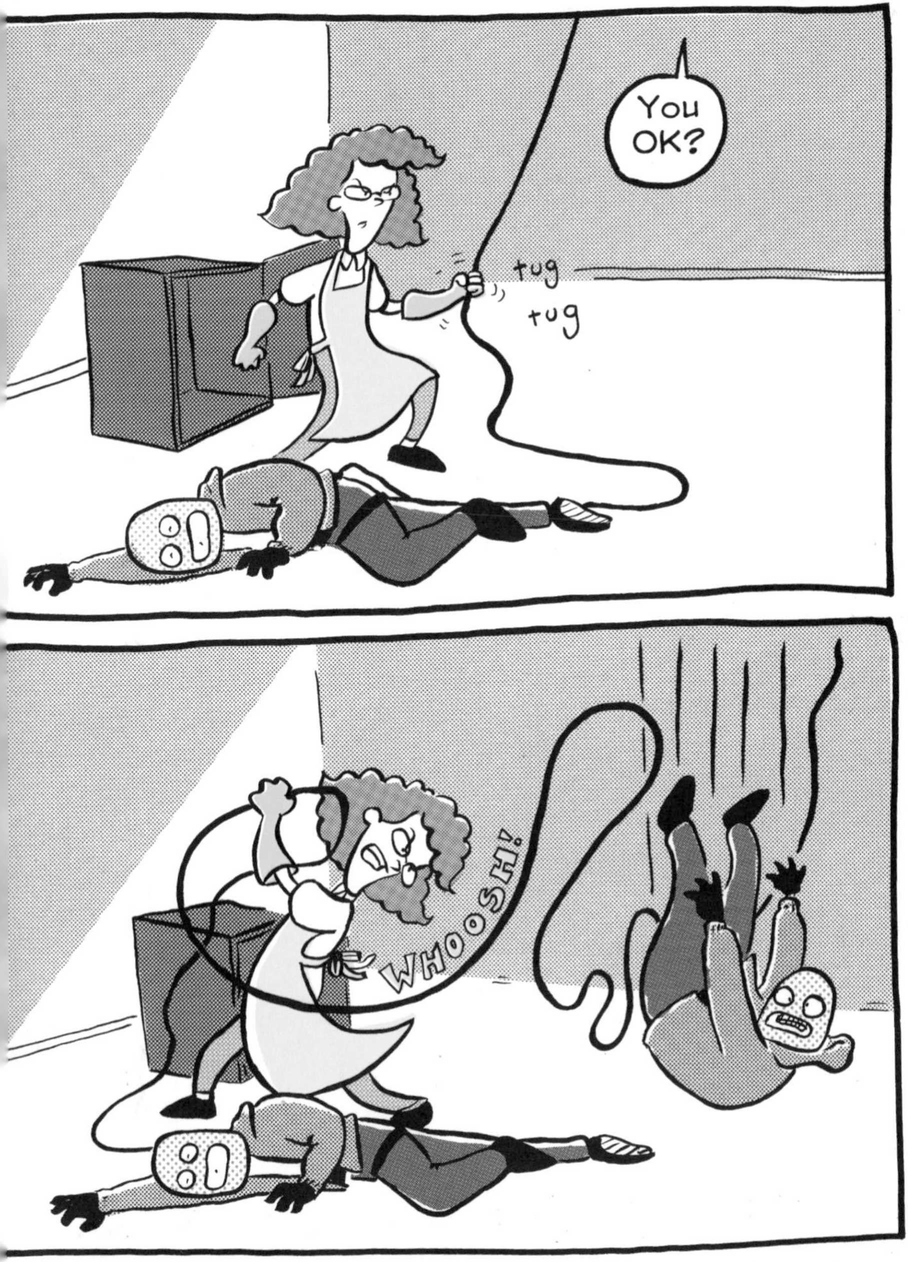
You OK?
tug
tug
WHOOSH!

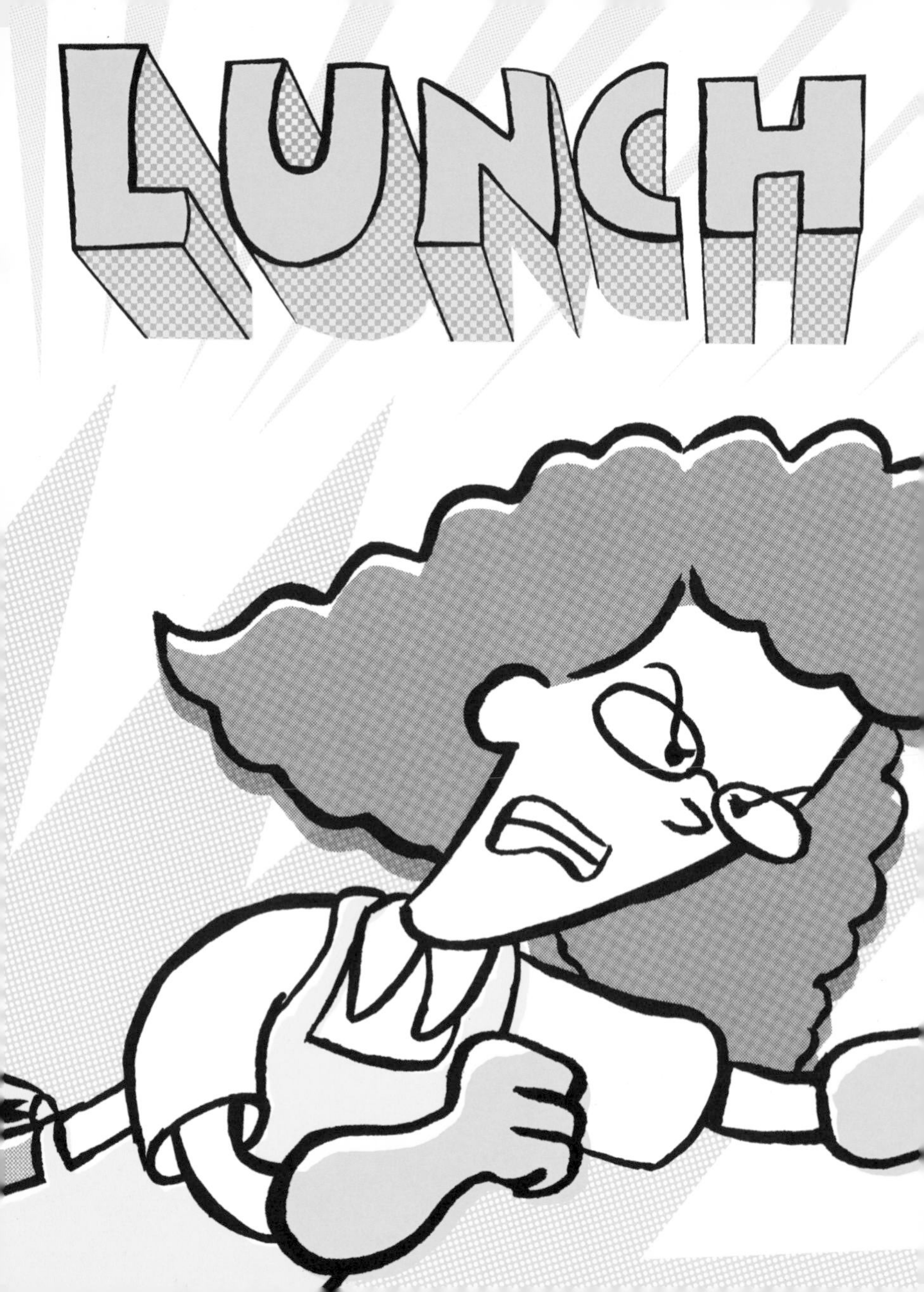
LUNCH

LADY

and the Bake Sale Bandit

Jarrett J. Krosoczka

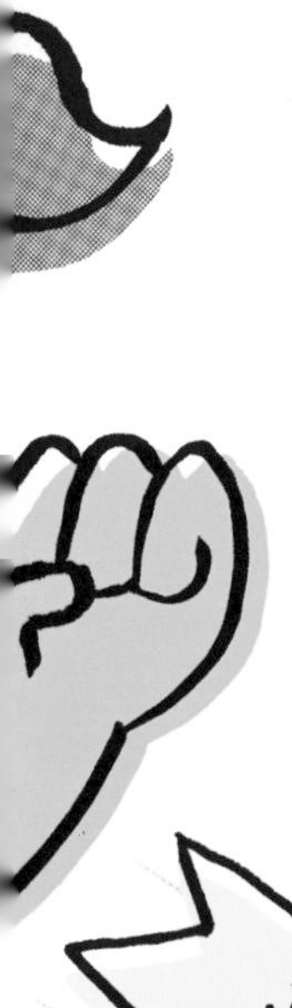

Alfred A. Knopf New York

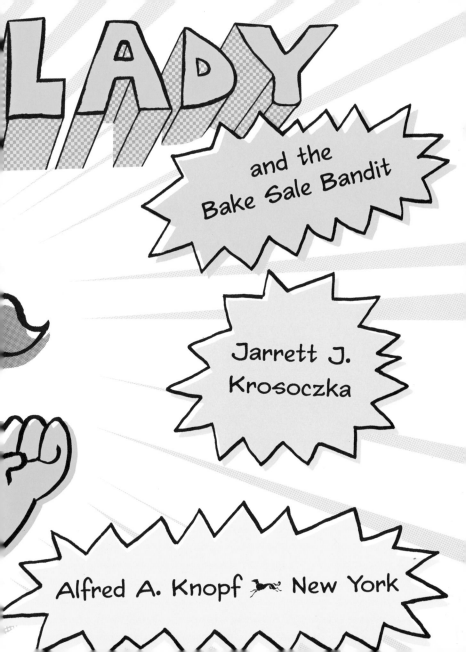

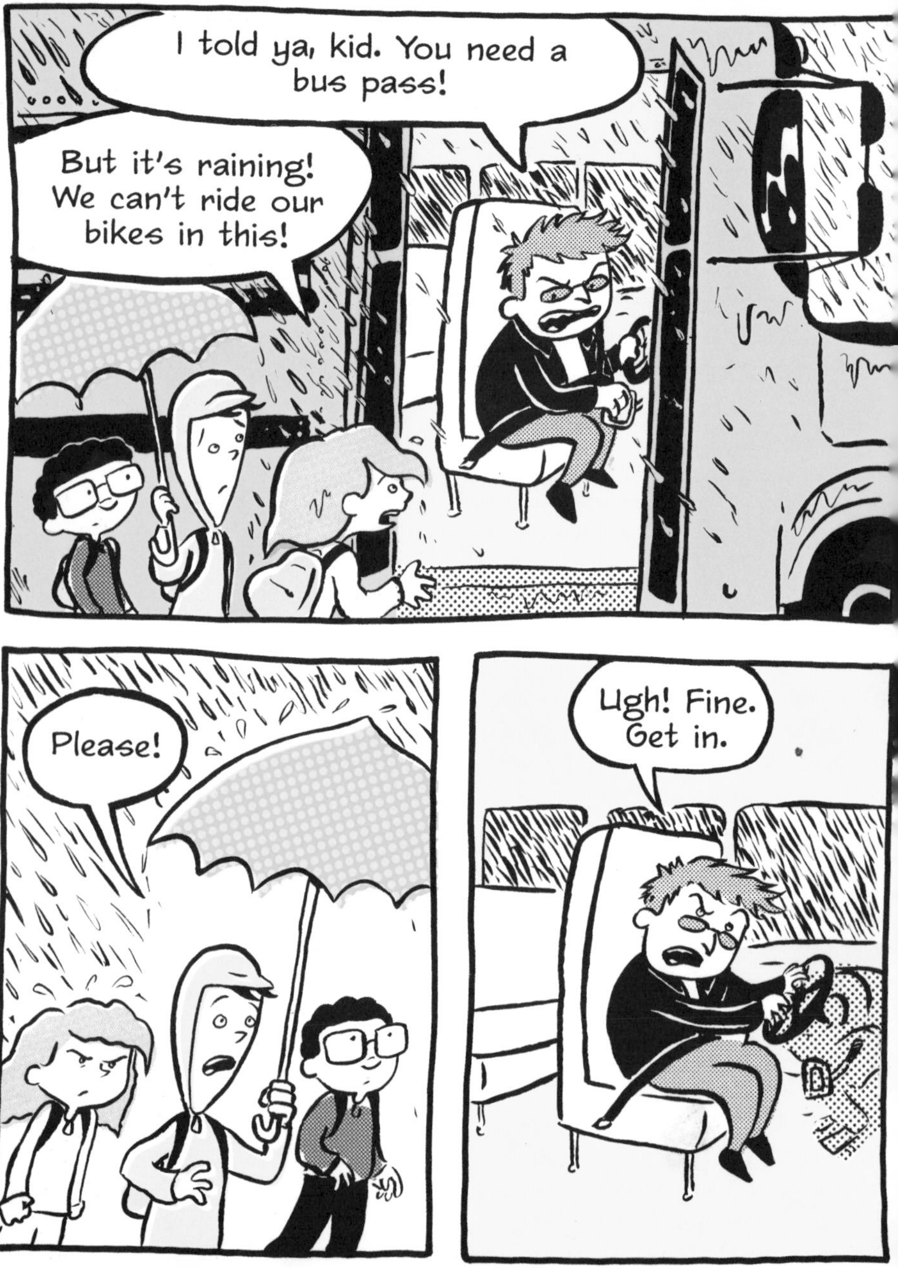
I told ya, kid. You need a bus pass!
But it's raining! We can't ride our bikes in this!
Please!
Ugh! Fine. Get in.

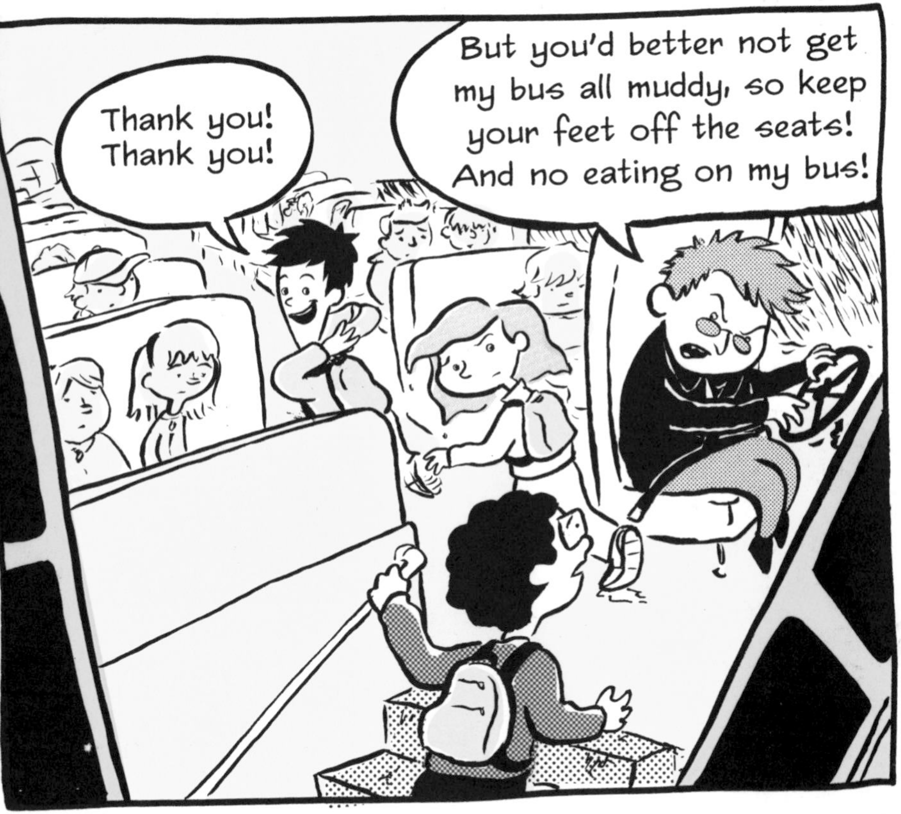
Thank you! Thank you!
But you'd better not get my bus all muddy, so keep your feet off the seats! And no eating on my bus!

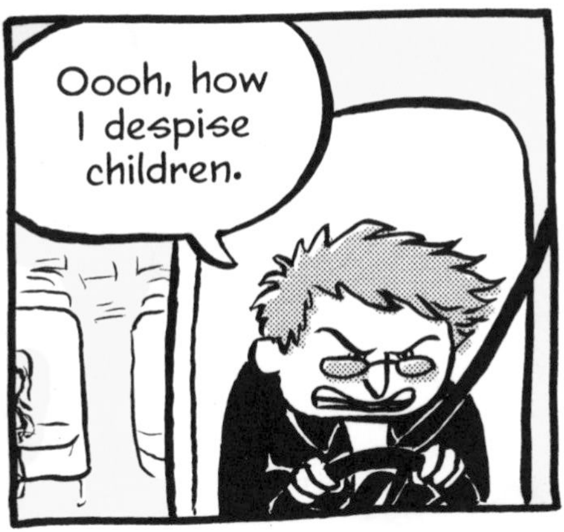
Oooh, how I despise children.

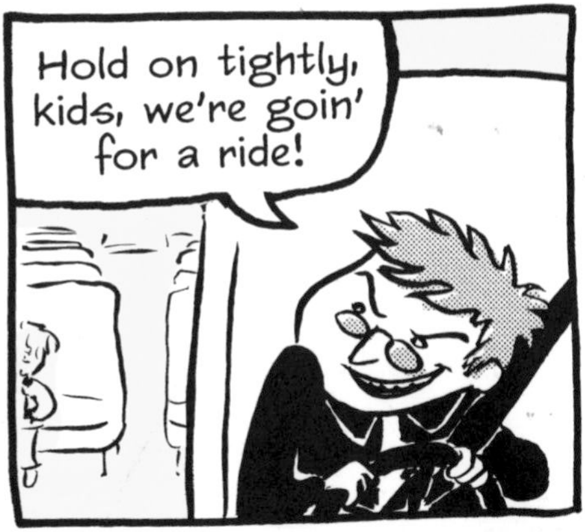
Hold on tightly, kids, we're goin' for a ride!

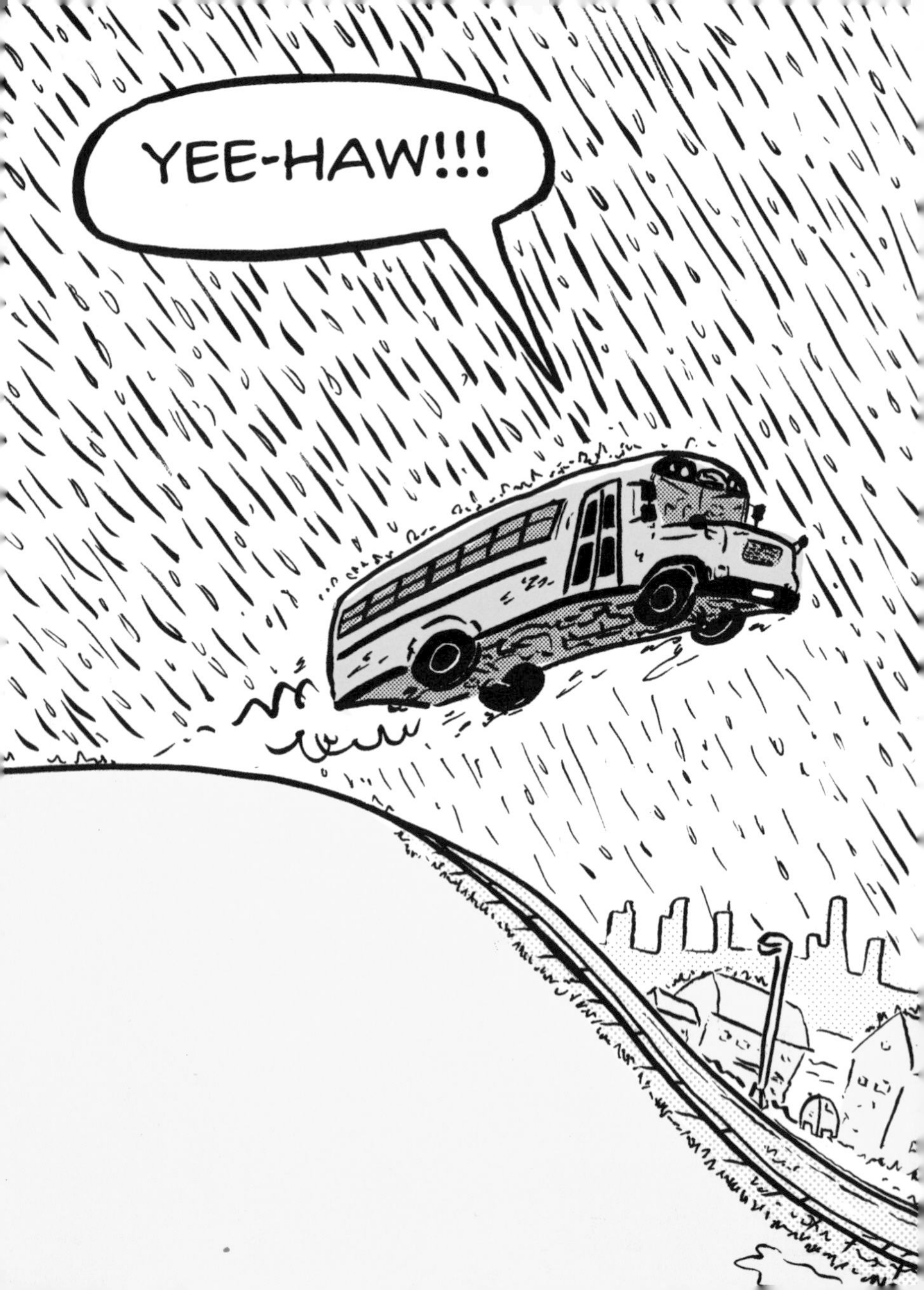
YEE-HAW!!!

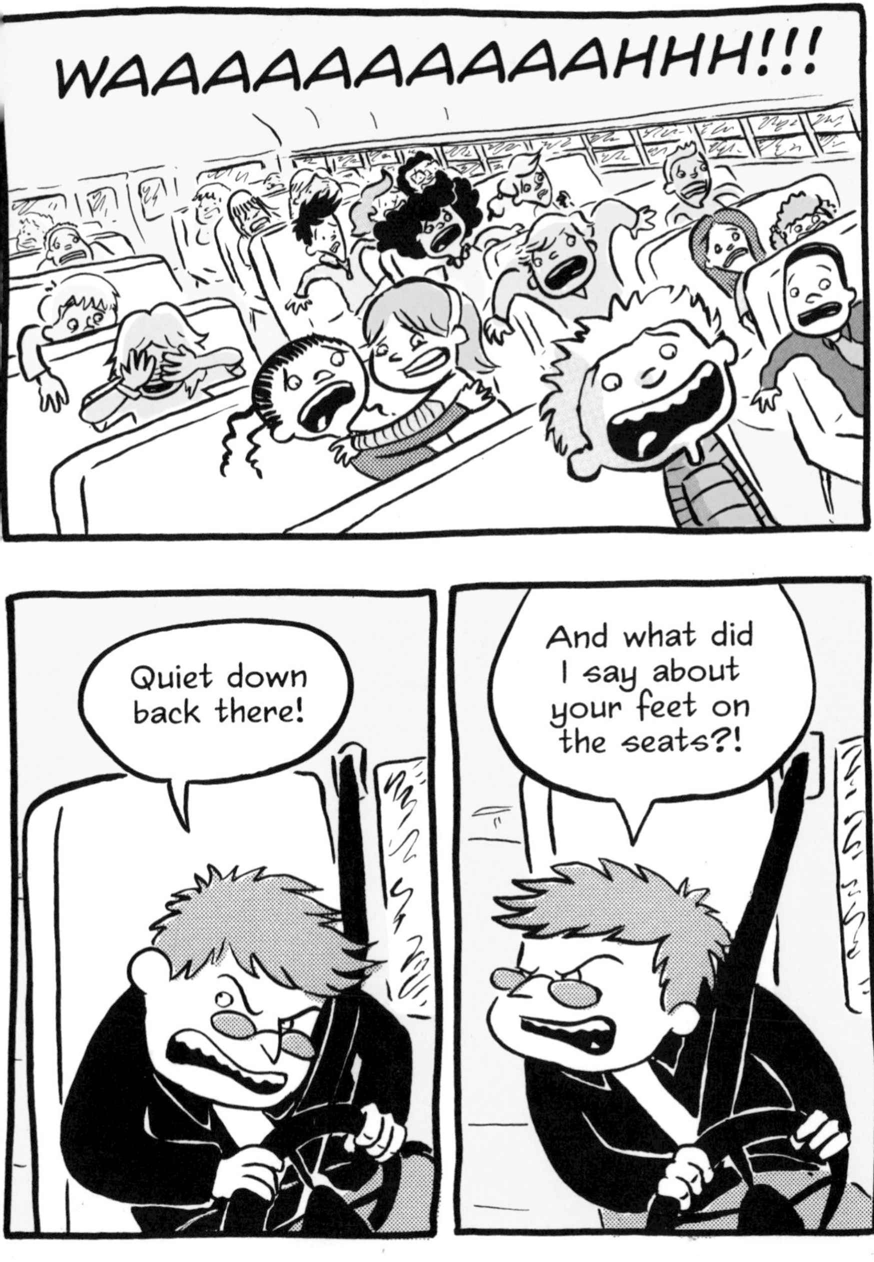
WAAAAAAAAAAHHH!!!
Quiet down back there!
And what did I say about your feet on the seats?!

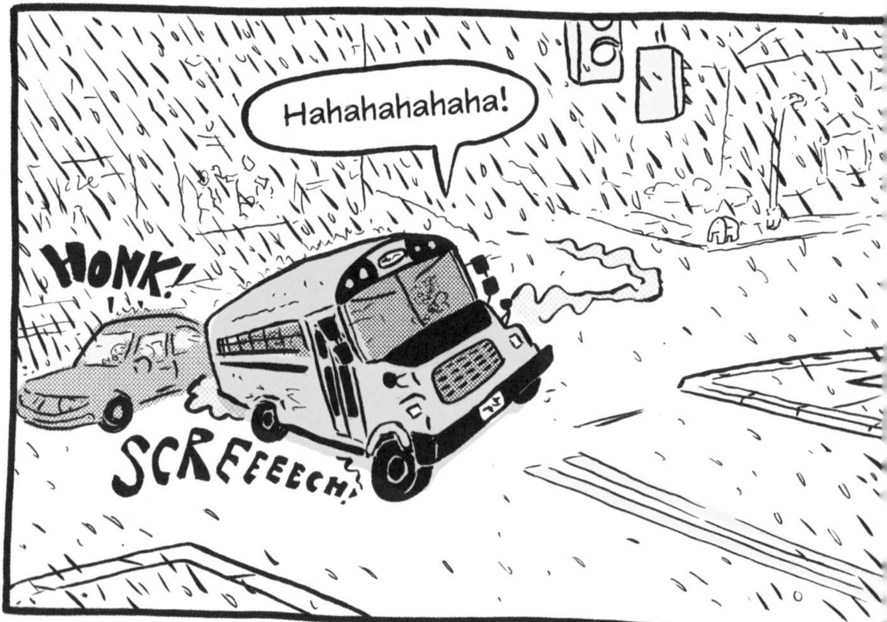
Hahahahahaha!
HONK!
SCREEEEECH!

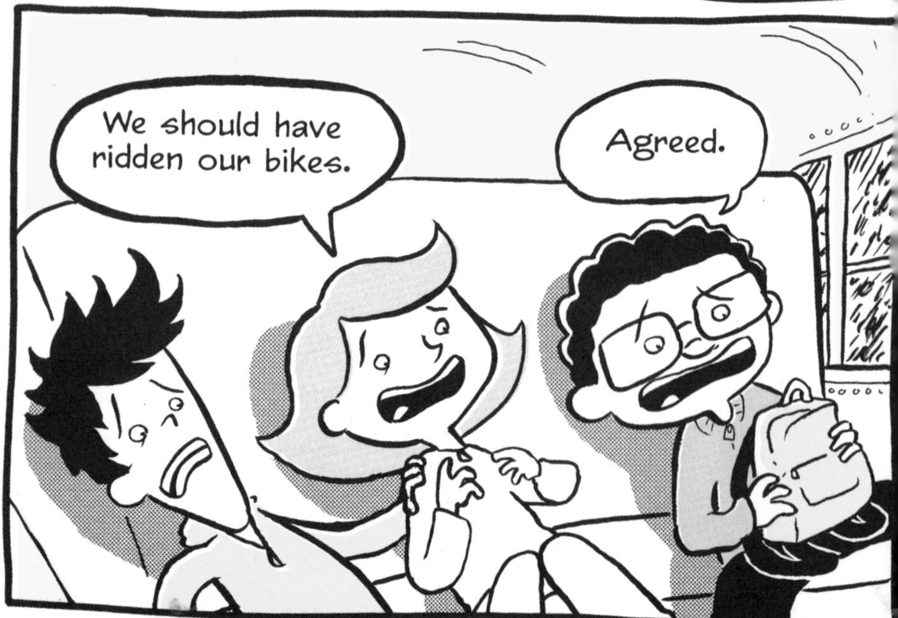
We should have ridden our bikes.
Agreed.

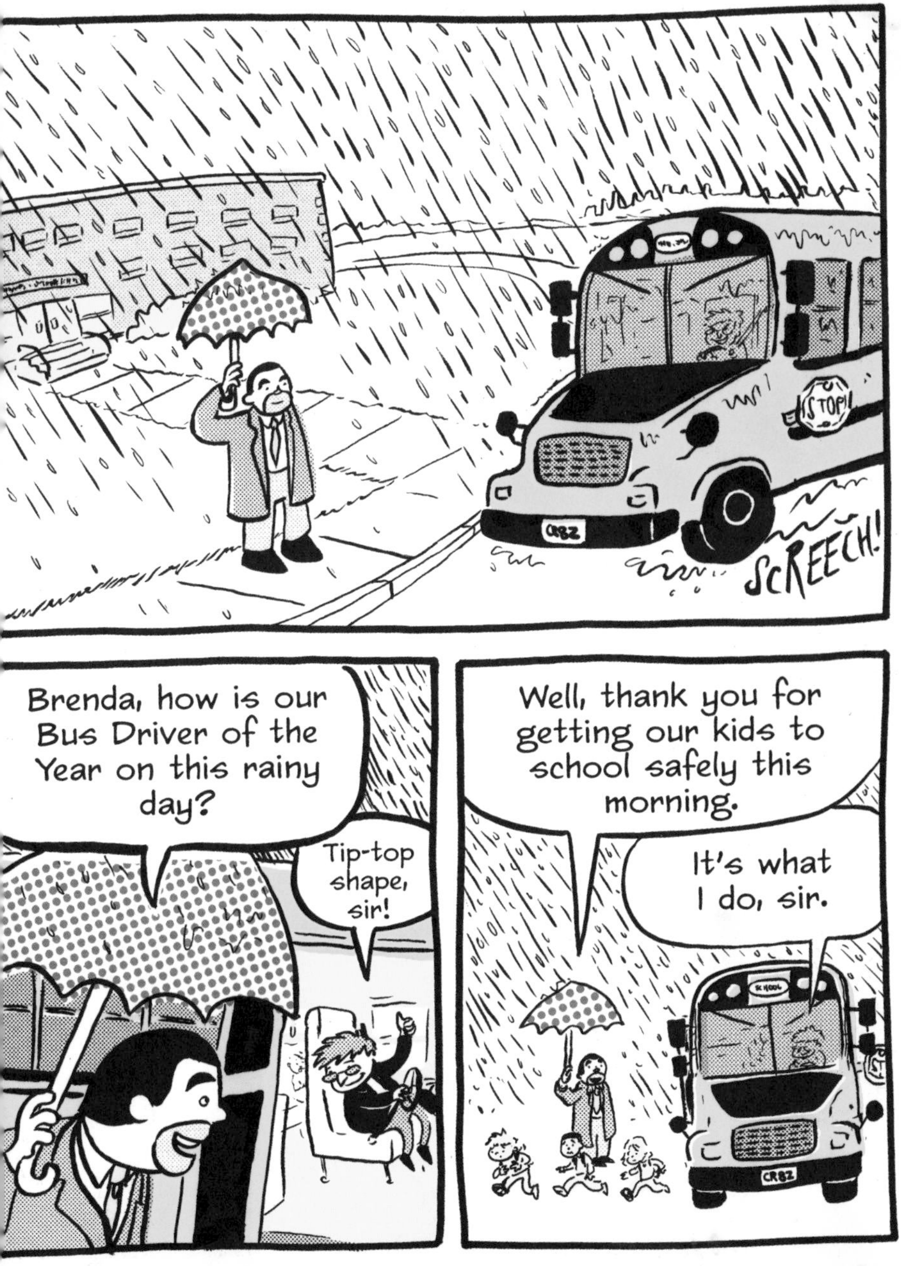
STOP!
SCREECH!
Brenda, how is our Bus Driver of the Year on this rainy day?
Tip-top shape, sir!
Well, thank you for getting our kids to school safely this morning.
It's what I do, sir.

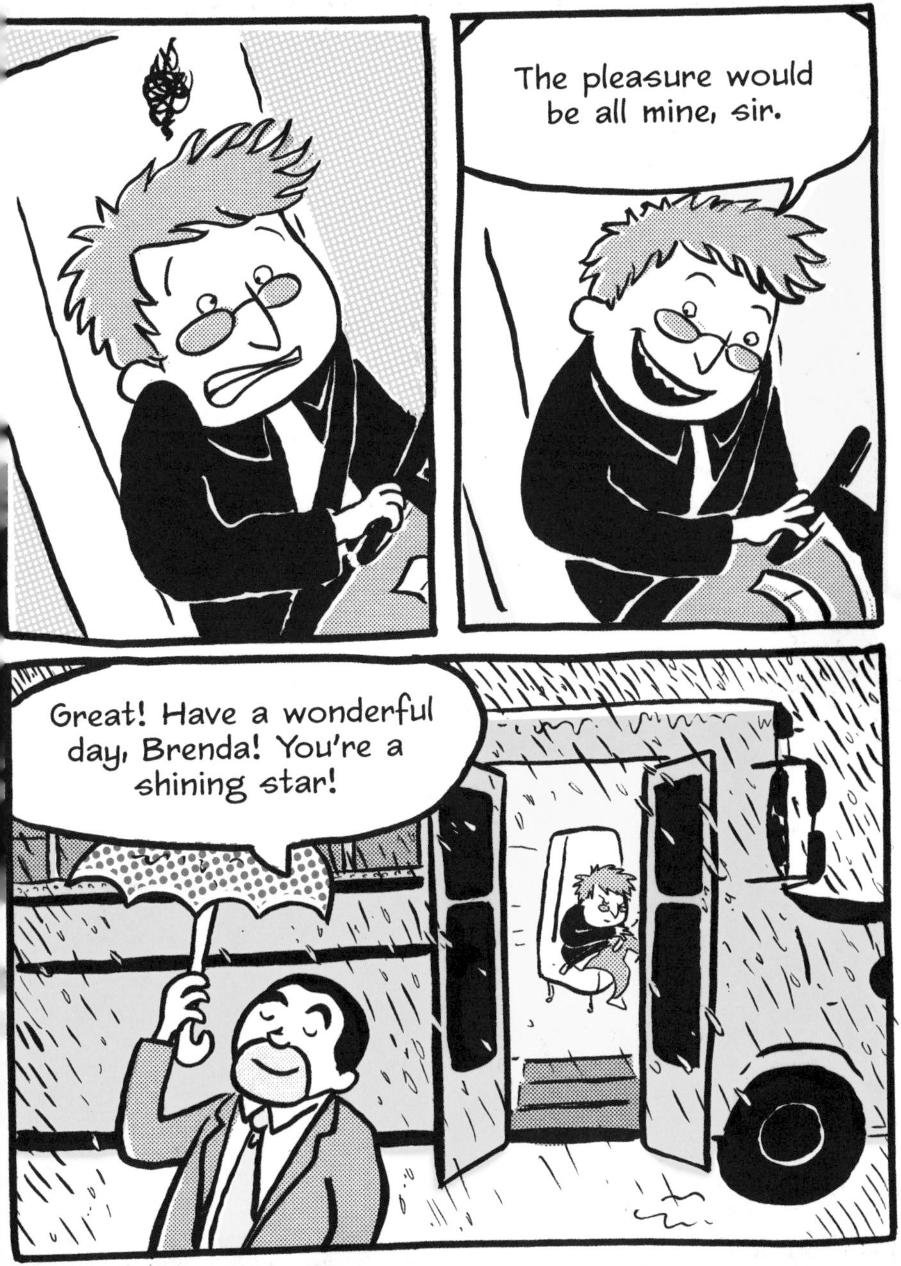
The pleasure would be all mine, sir.
Great! Have a wonderful day, Brenda! You're a shining star!

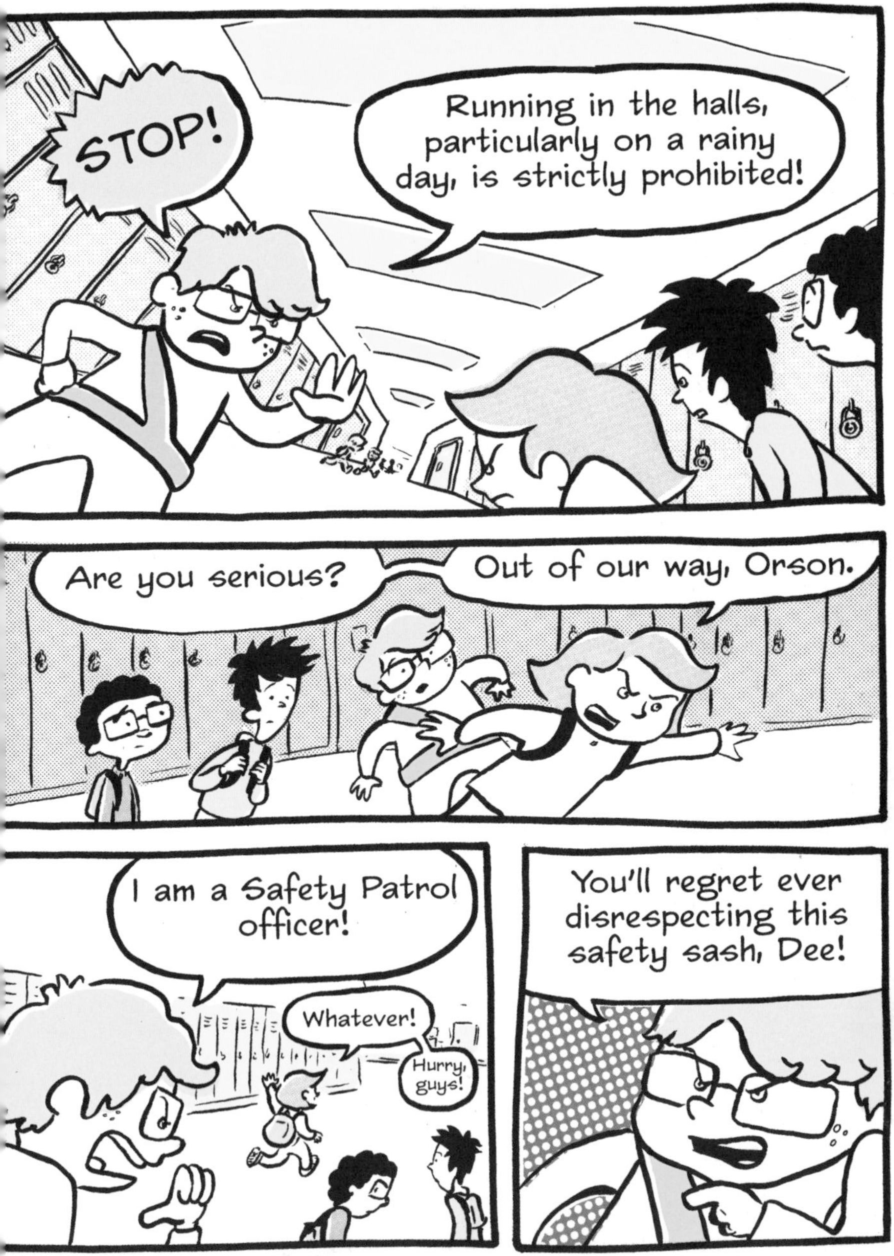
STOP!
Running in the halls, particularly on a rainy day, is strictly prohibited!
Are you serious?
Out of our way, Orson.
I am a Safety Patrol officer!
Whatever!
Hurry, guys!
You'll regret ever disrespecting this safety sash, Dee!

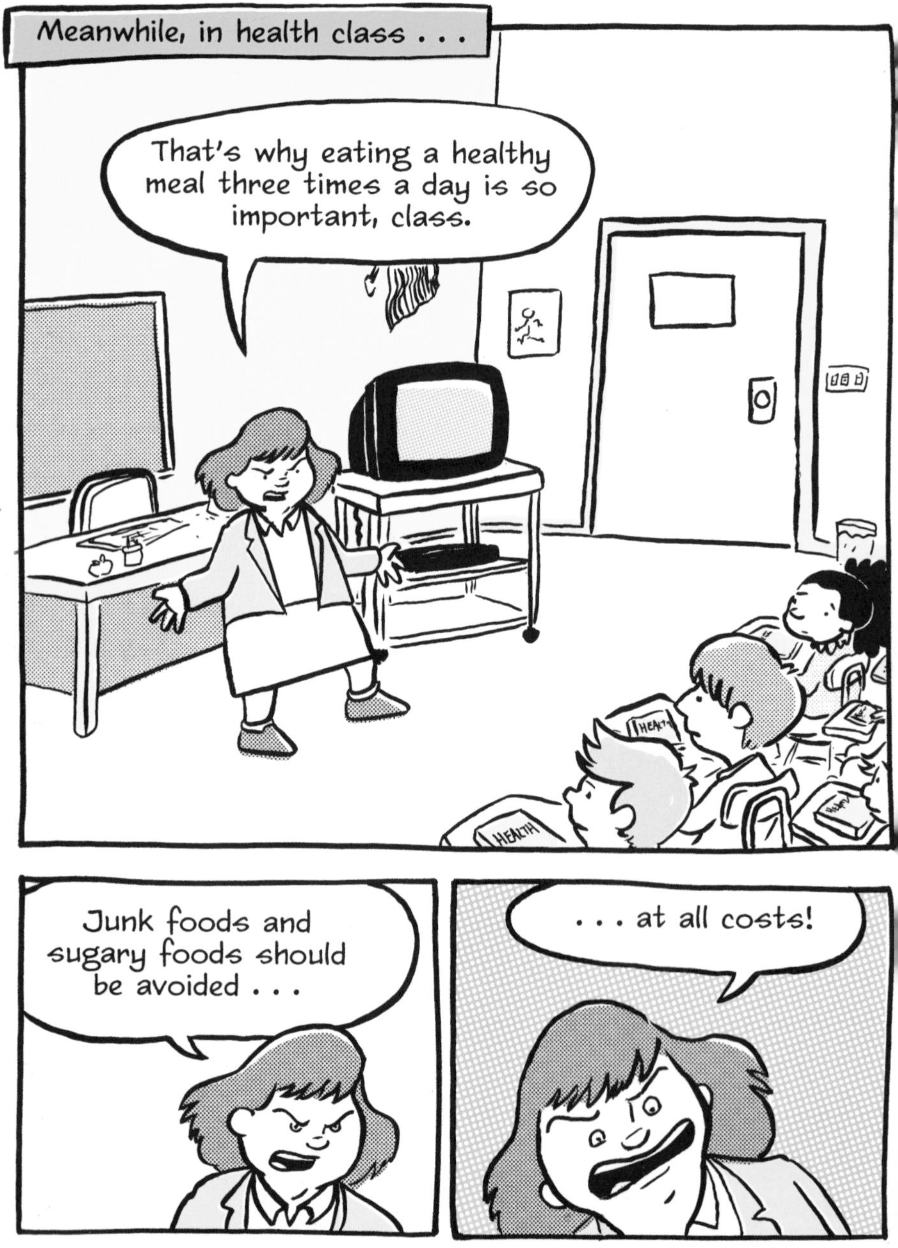
Meanwhile, in health class . . .
That's why eating a healthy meal three times a day is so important, class.
HEALTH
Junk foods and sugary foods should be avoided . . .
. . . at all costs!

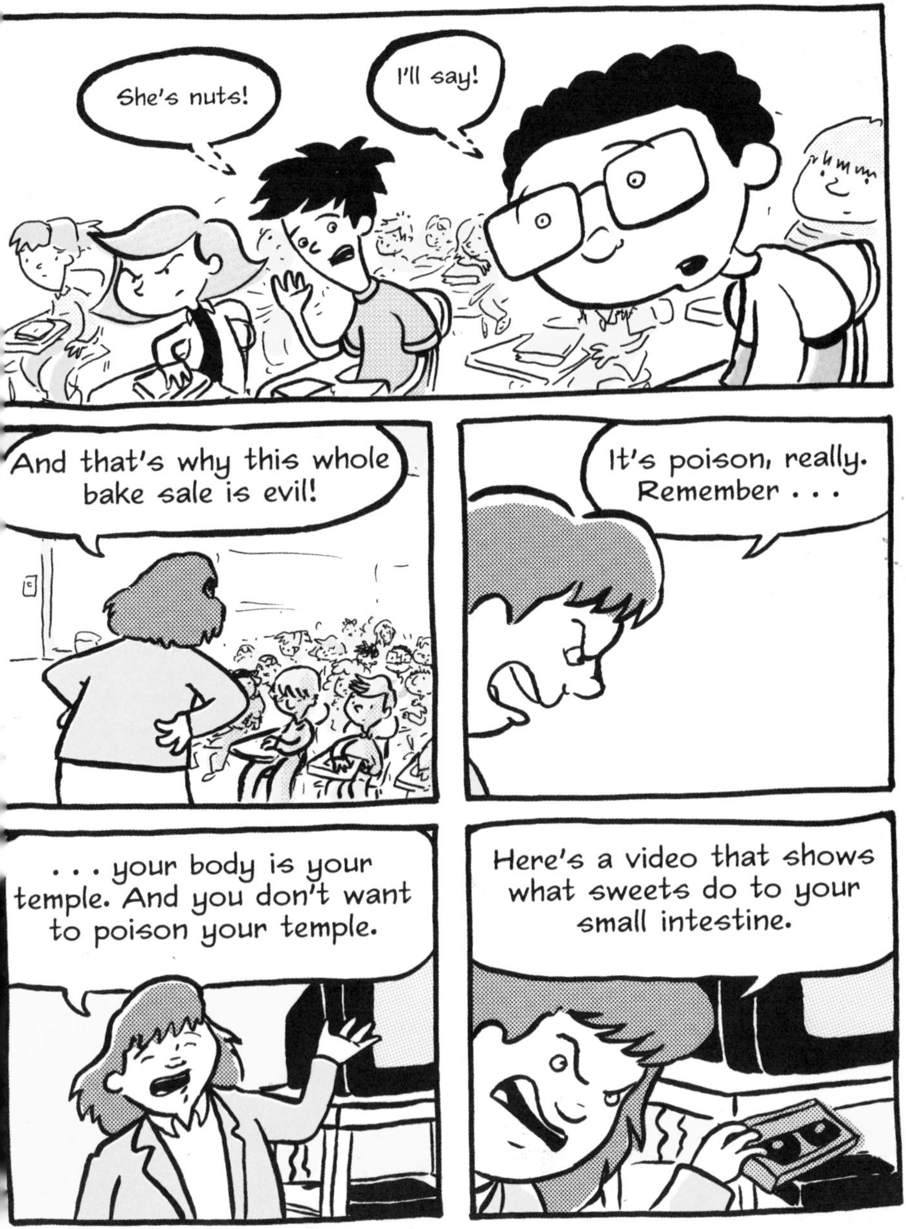
She's nuts!
I'll say!
And that's why this whole bake sale is evil!
It's poison, really. Remember . . .
. . . your body is your temple. And you don't want to poison your temple.
Here's a video that shows what sweets do to your small intestine.

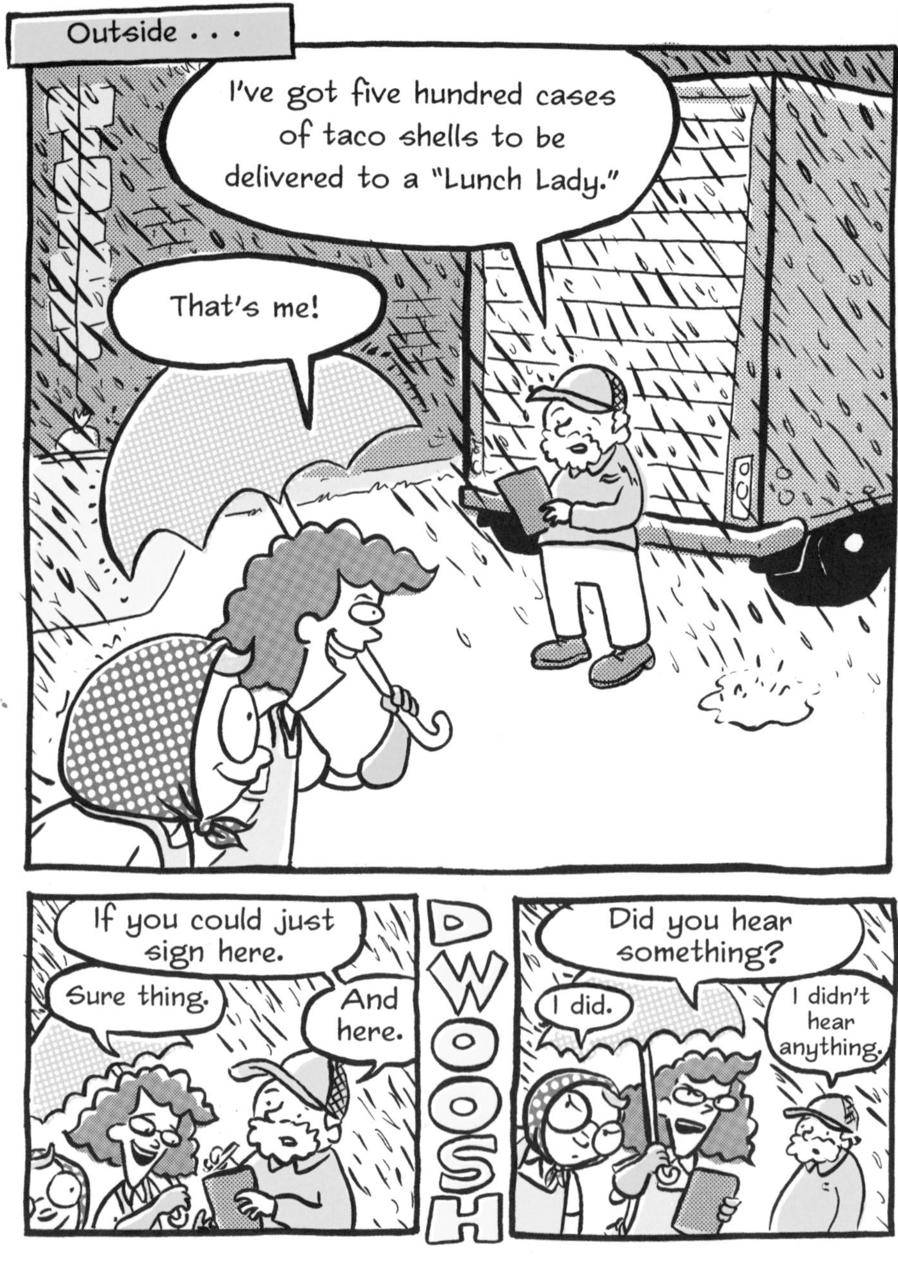
Outside . . .
I've got five hundred cases of taco shells to be delivered to a "Lunch Lady."
That's me!
If you could just sign here.
Sure thing.
And here.
DWOOOSH
Did you hear something?
I did.
I didn't hear anything.

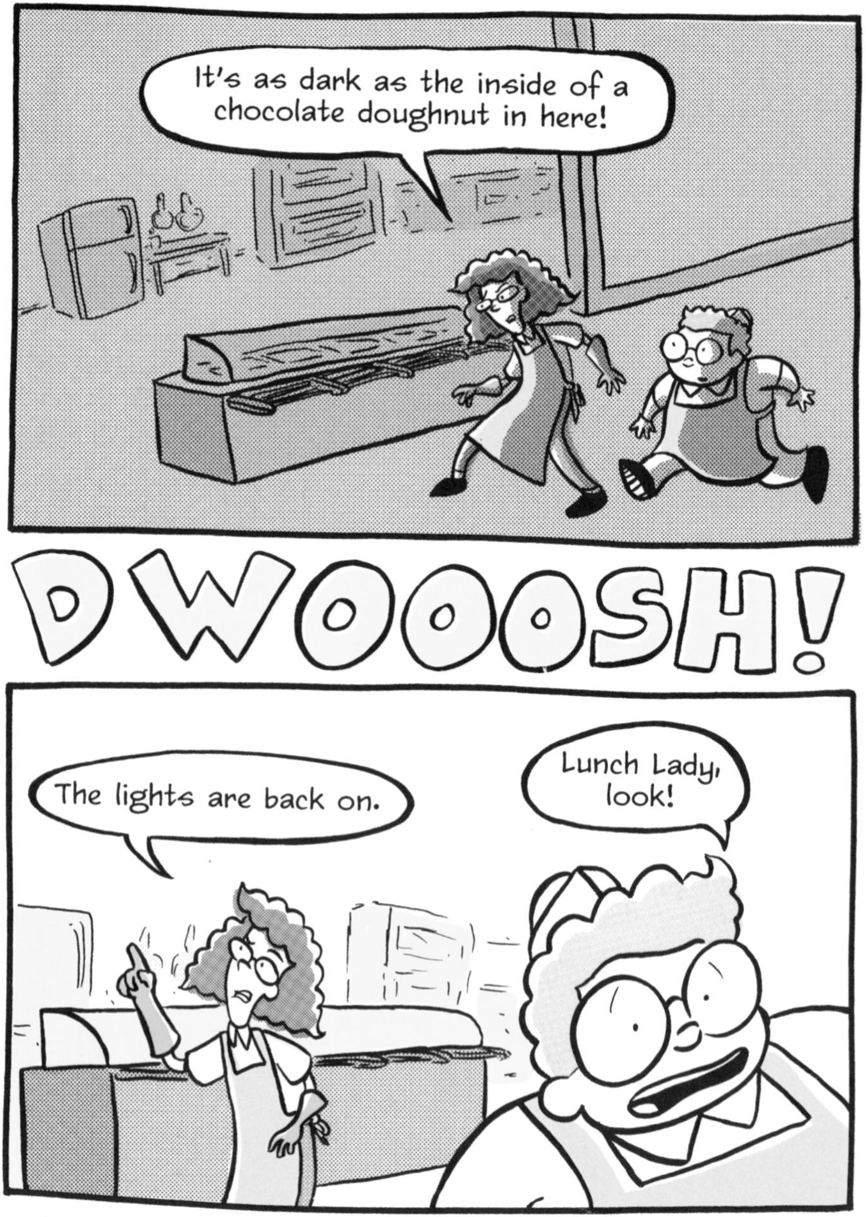
It's as dark as the inside of a chocolate doughnut in here!
DWOOOSH!
The lights are back on.
Lunch Lady, look!

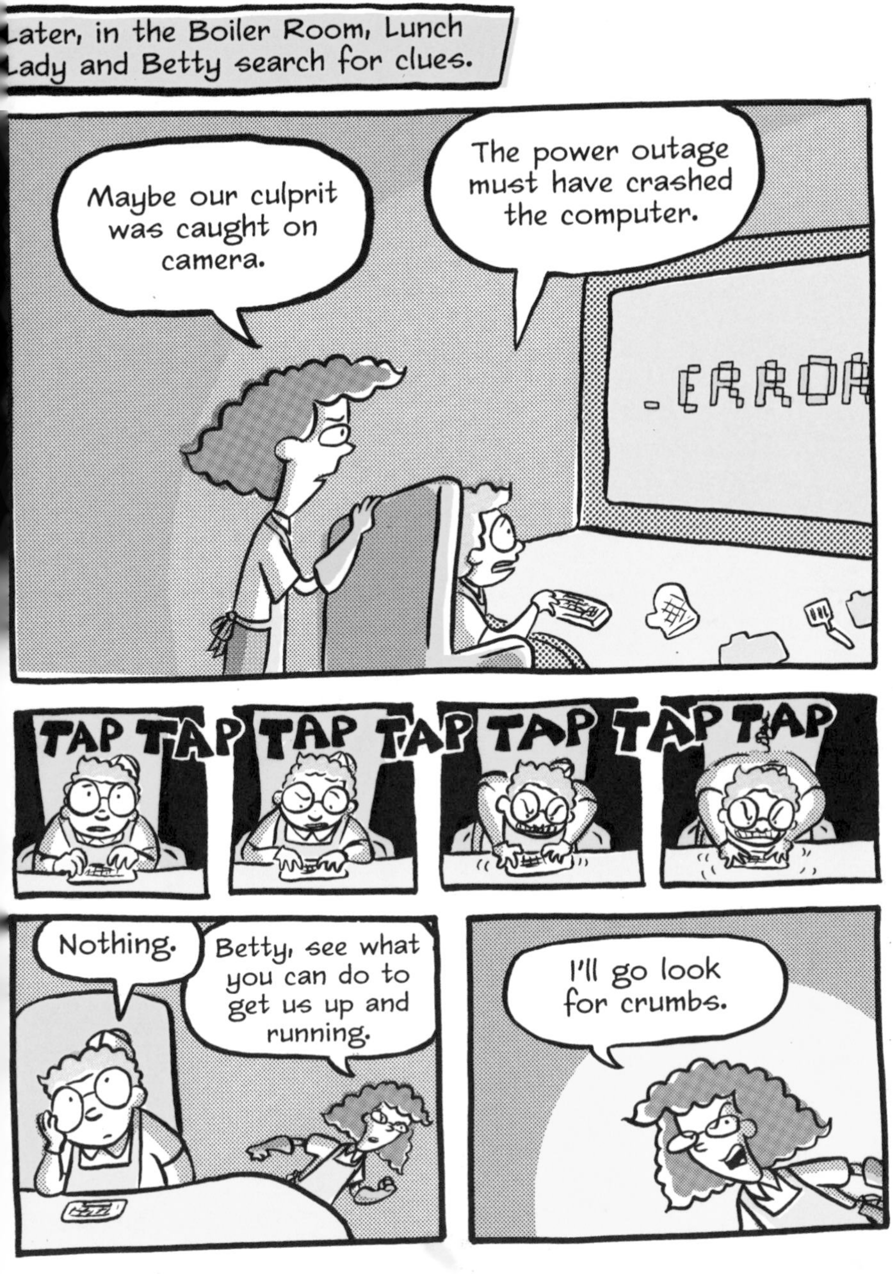
Later, in the Boiler Room, Lunch Lady and Betty search for clues.
Maybe our culprit was caught on camera.
The power outage must have crashed the computer.
ERROR
TAP TAP TAP TAP TAP TAP TAP
Nothing.
Betty, see what you can do to get us up and running.
I'll go look for crumbs.

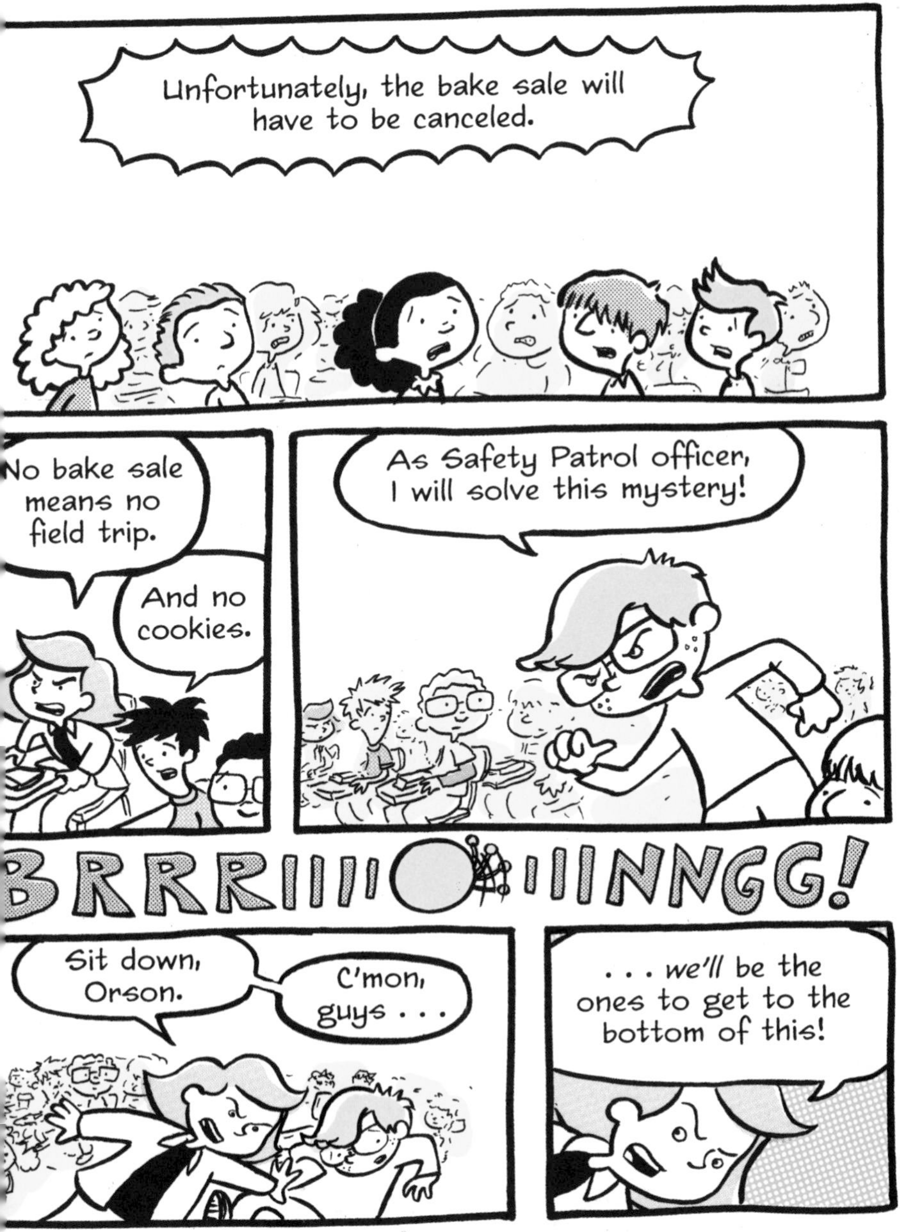
Unfortunately, the bake sale will have to be canceled.
No bake sale means no field trip.
And no cookies.
As Safety Patrol officer, I will solve this mystery!
BRRRIIII IIINNGG!
Sit down, Orson.
C'mon, guys . . .
. . . *we'll* be the ones to get to the bottom of this!

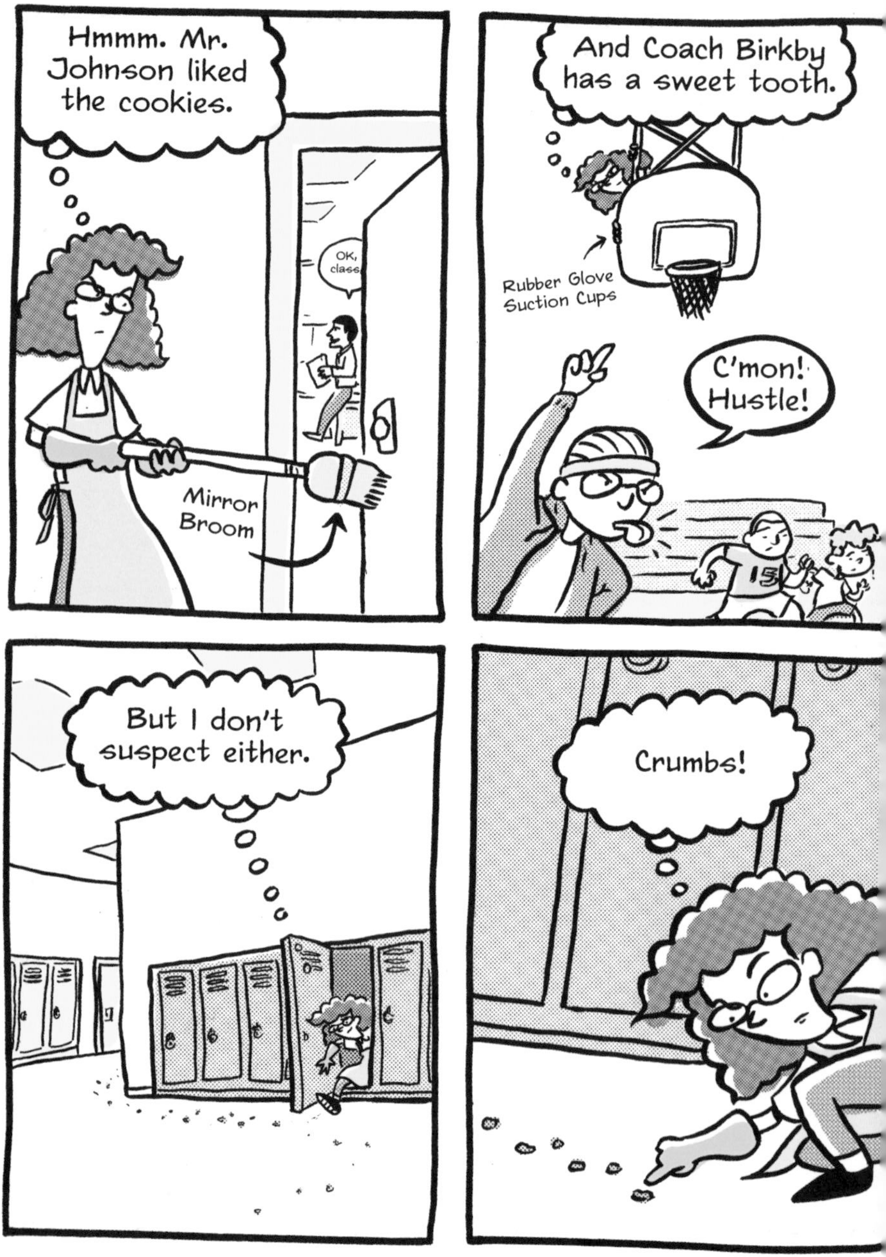
Hmmm. Mr. Johnson liked the cookies.
OK, class
Mirror Broom
And Coach Birkby has a sweet tooth.
Rubber Glove Suction Cups
C'mon! Hustle!
15
But I don't suspect either.
Crumbs!

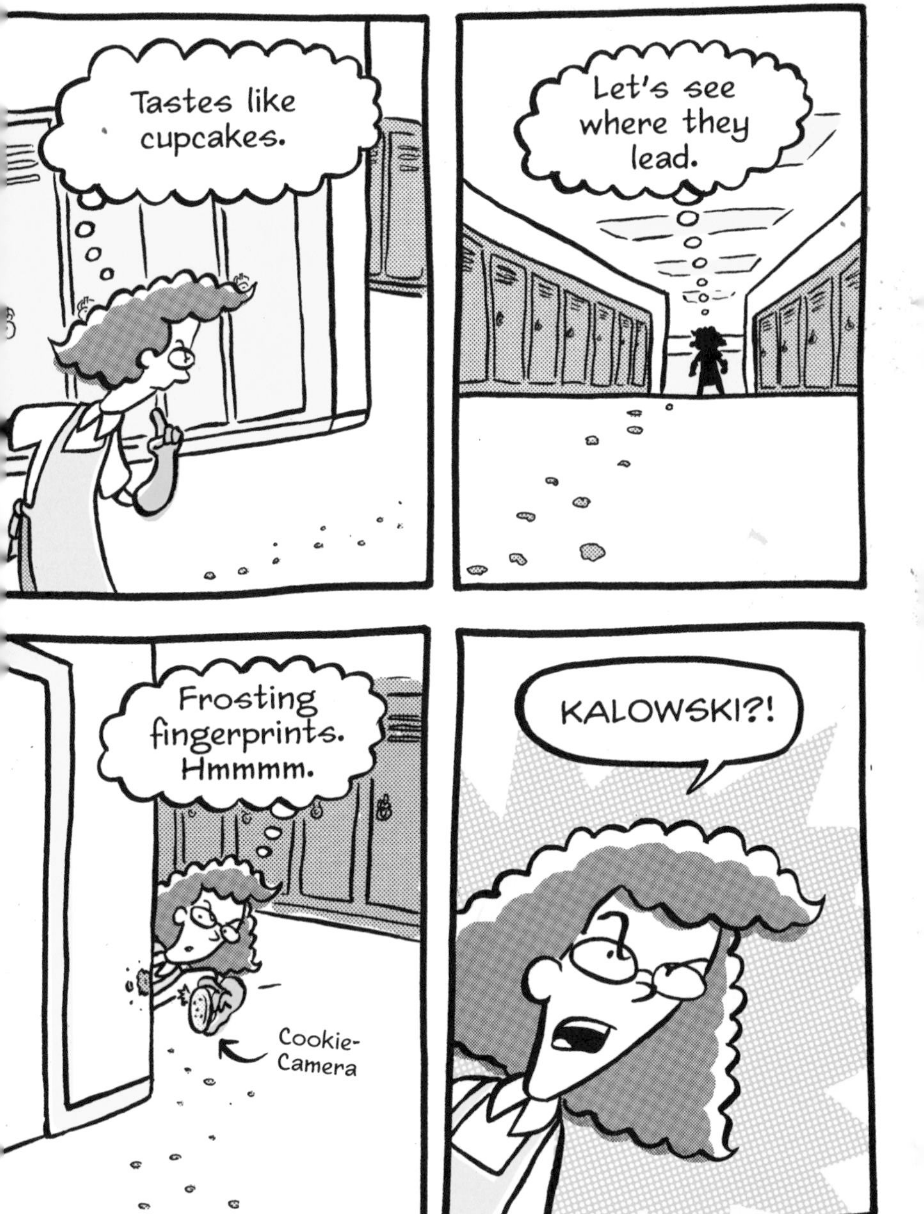
Tastes like cupcakes.
Let's see where they lead.
Frosting fingerprints. Hmmmm.
Cookie-Camera
KALOWSKI?!

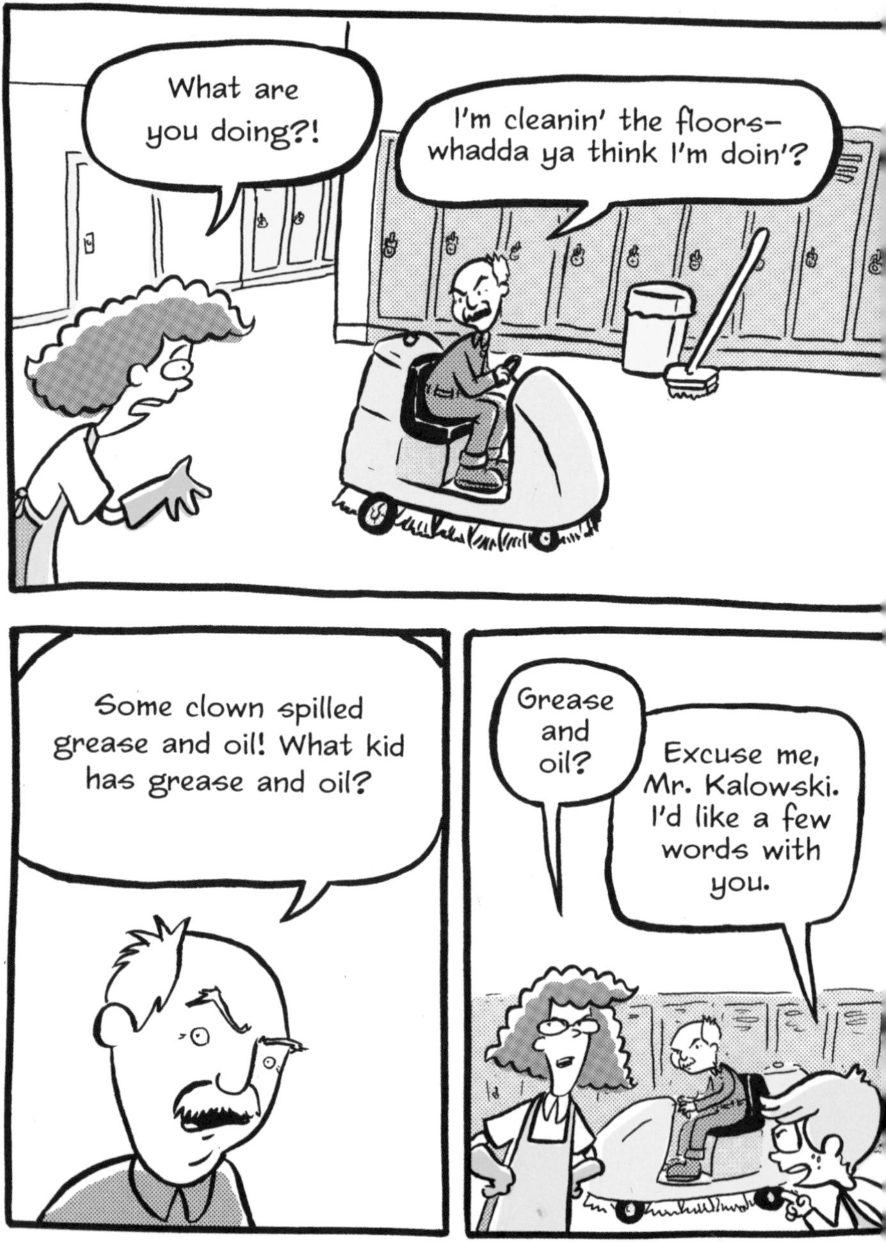
What are you doing?!
I'm cleanin' the floors— whadda ya think I'm doin'?
Some clown spilled grease and oil! What kid has grease and oil?
Grease and oil?
Excuse me, Mr. Kalowski. I'd like a few words with you.

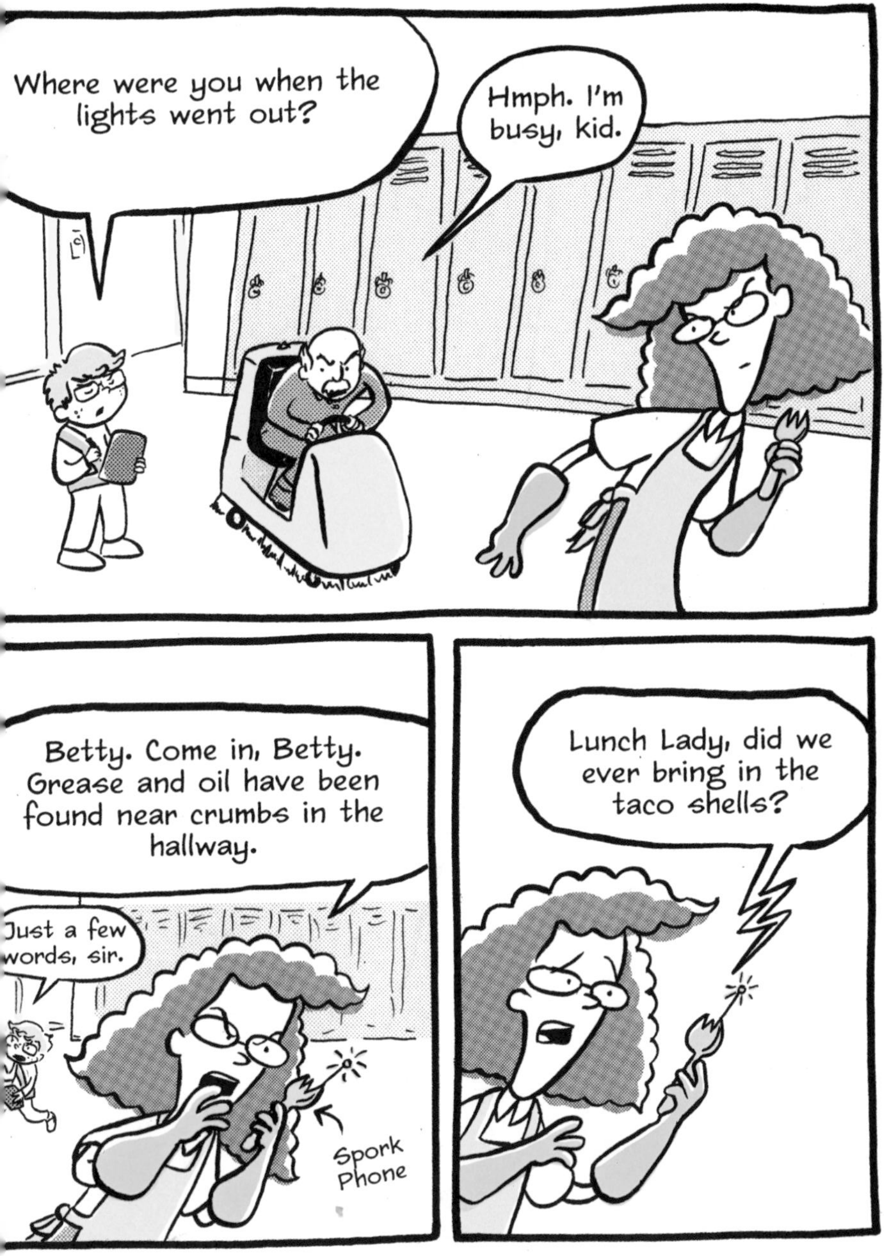

Where were you when the lights went out?
Hmph. I'm busy, kid.
Betty. Come in, Betty. Grease and oil have been found near crumbs in the hallway.
Just a few words, sir.
Spork Phone
Lunch Lady, did we ever bring in the taco shells?

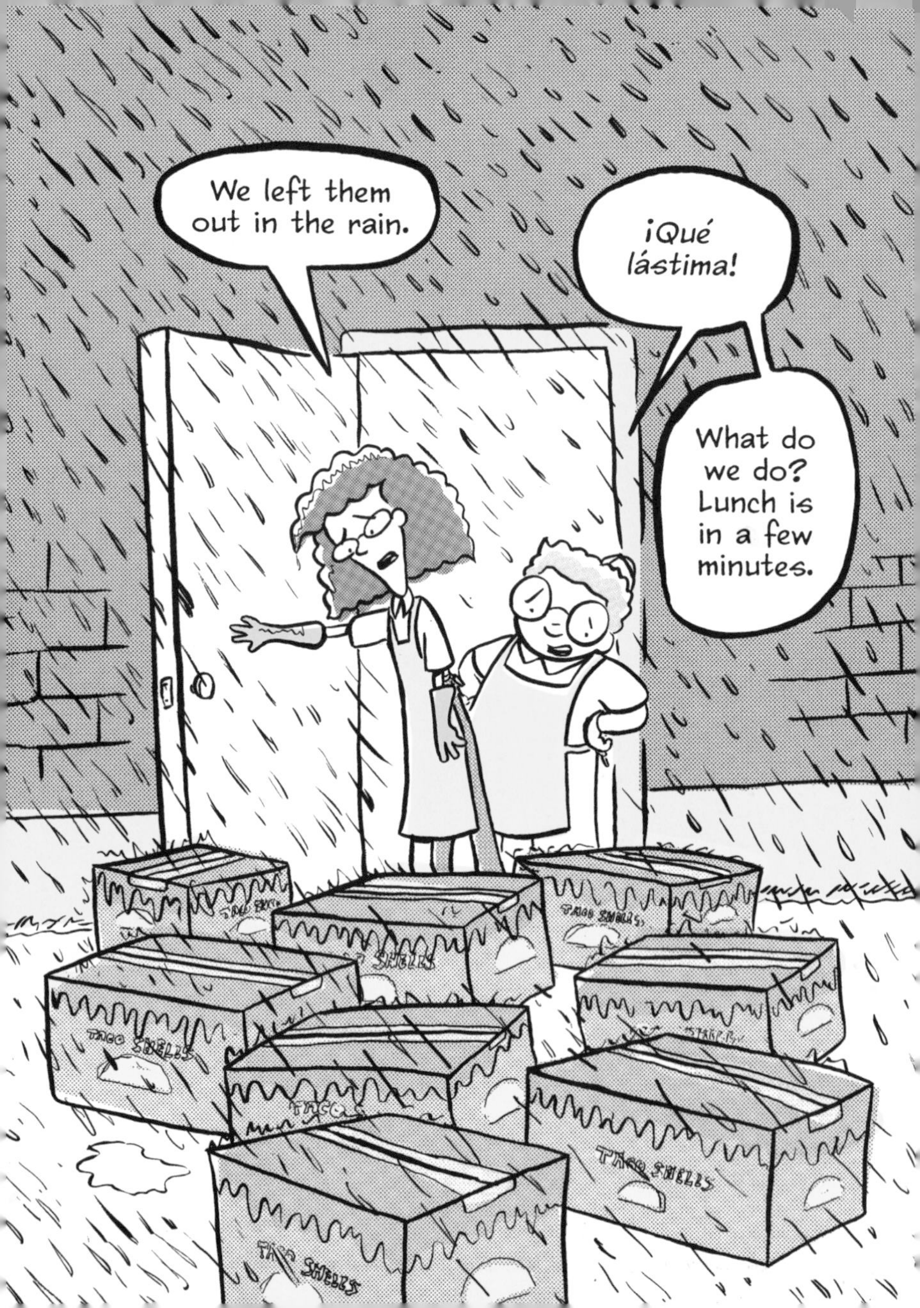
We left them out in the rain.
¡Qué lástima!
What do we do? Lunch is in a few minutes.
TACO SHELLS

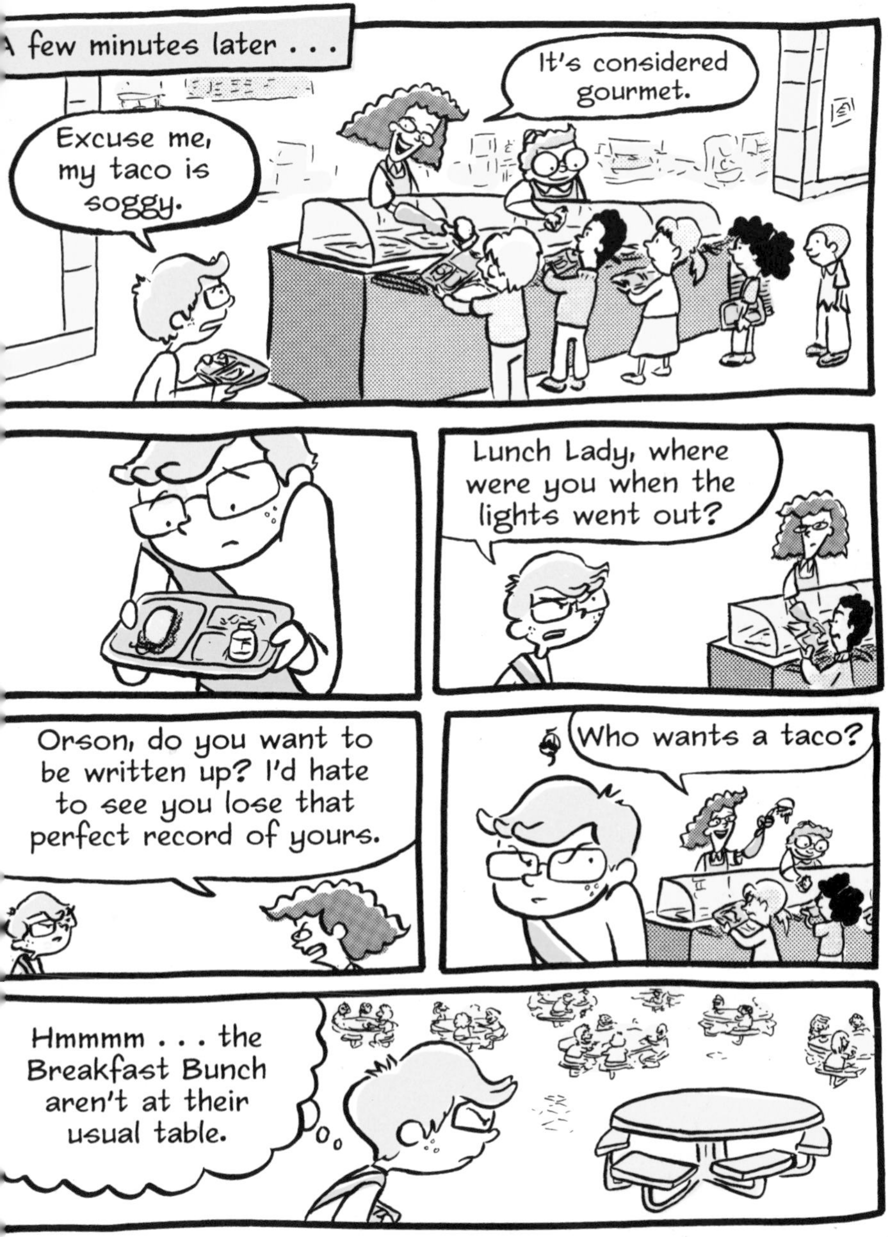
A few minutes later . . .
Excuse me, my taco is soggy.
It's considered gourmet.
Lunch Lady, where were you when the lights went out?
Orson, do you want to be written up? I'd hate to see you lose that perfect record of yours.
Who wants a taco?
Hmmmm . . . the Breakfast Bunch aren't at their usual table.

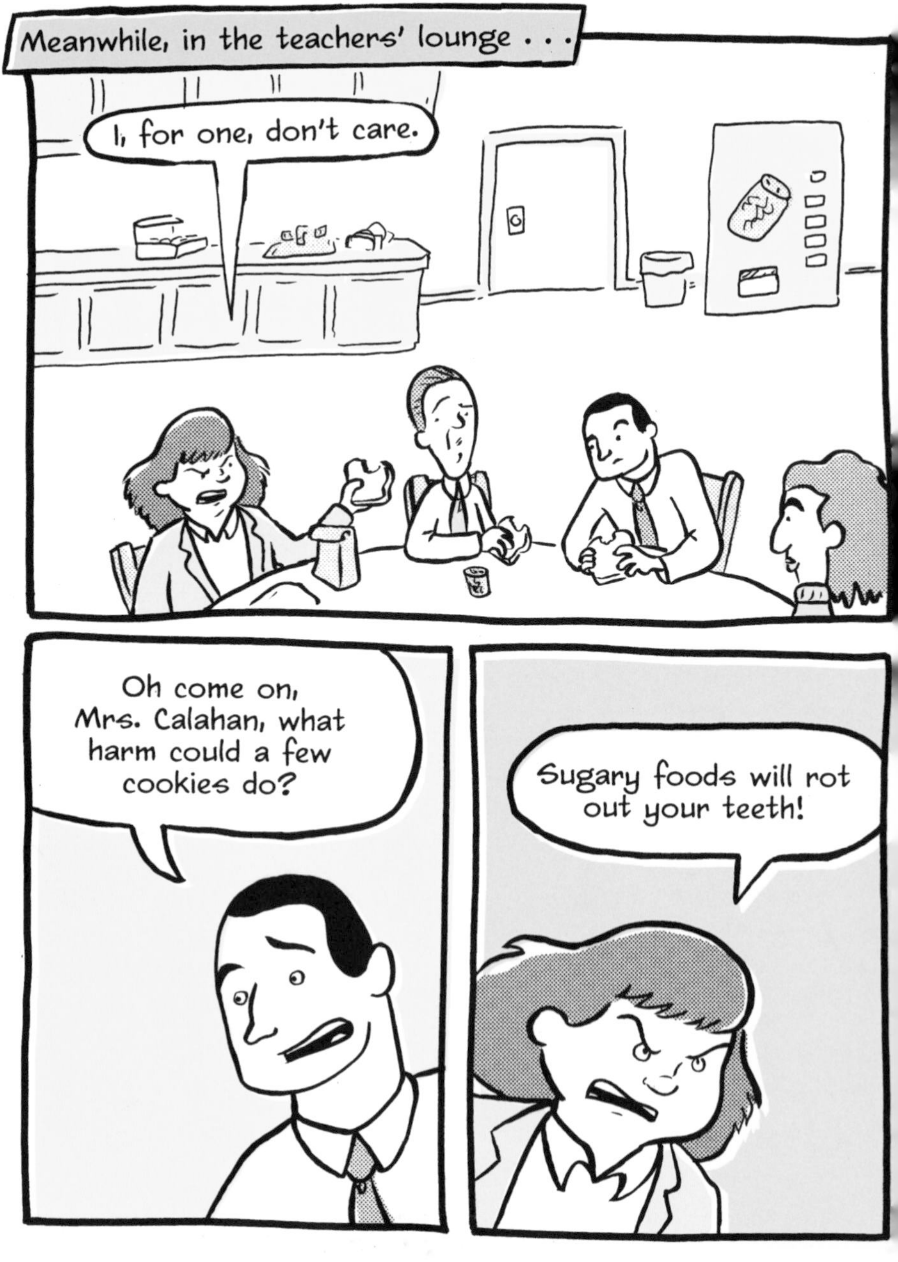
Meanwhile, in the teachers' lounge . . .
I, for one, don't care.
Oh come on, Mrs. Calahan, what harm could a few cookies do?
Sugary foods will rot out your teeth!

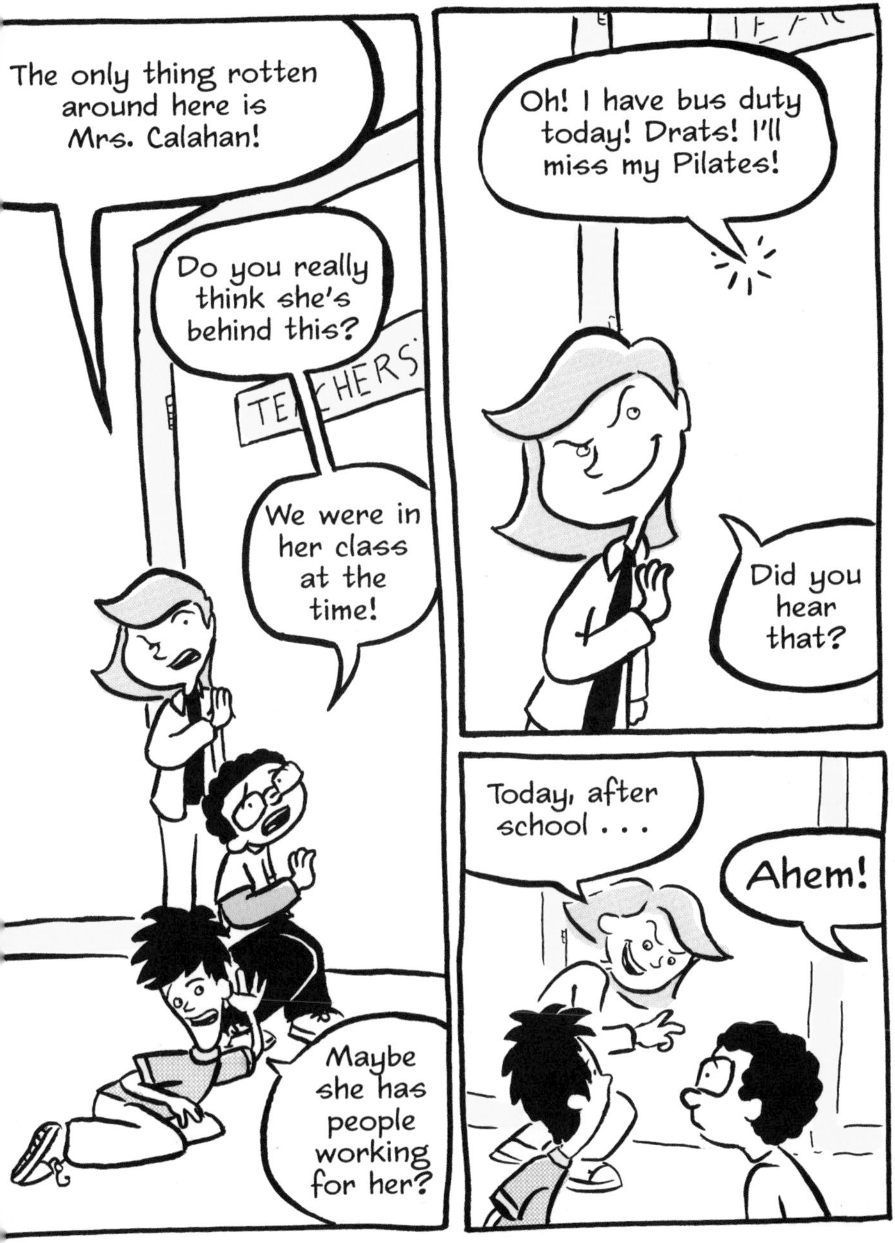

The only thing rotten around here is Mrs. Calahan!
Do you really think she's behind this?
TEACHERS'
We were in her class at the time!
Maybe she has people working for her?
Oh! I have bus duty today! Drats! I'll miss my Pilates!
Did you hear that?
Today, after school . . .
Ahem!

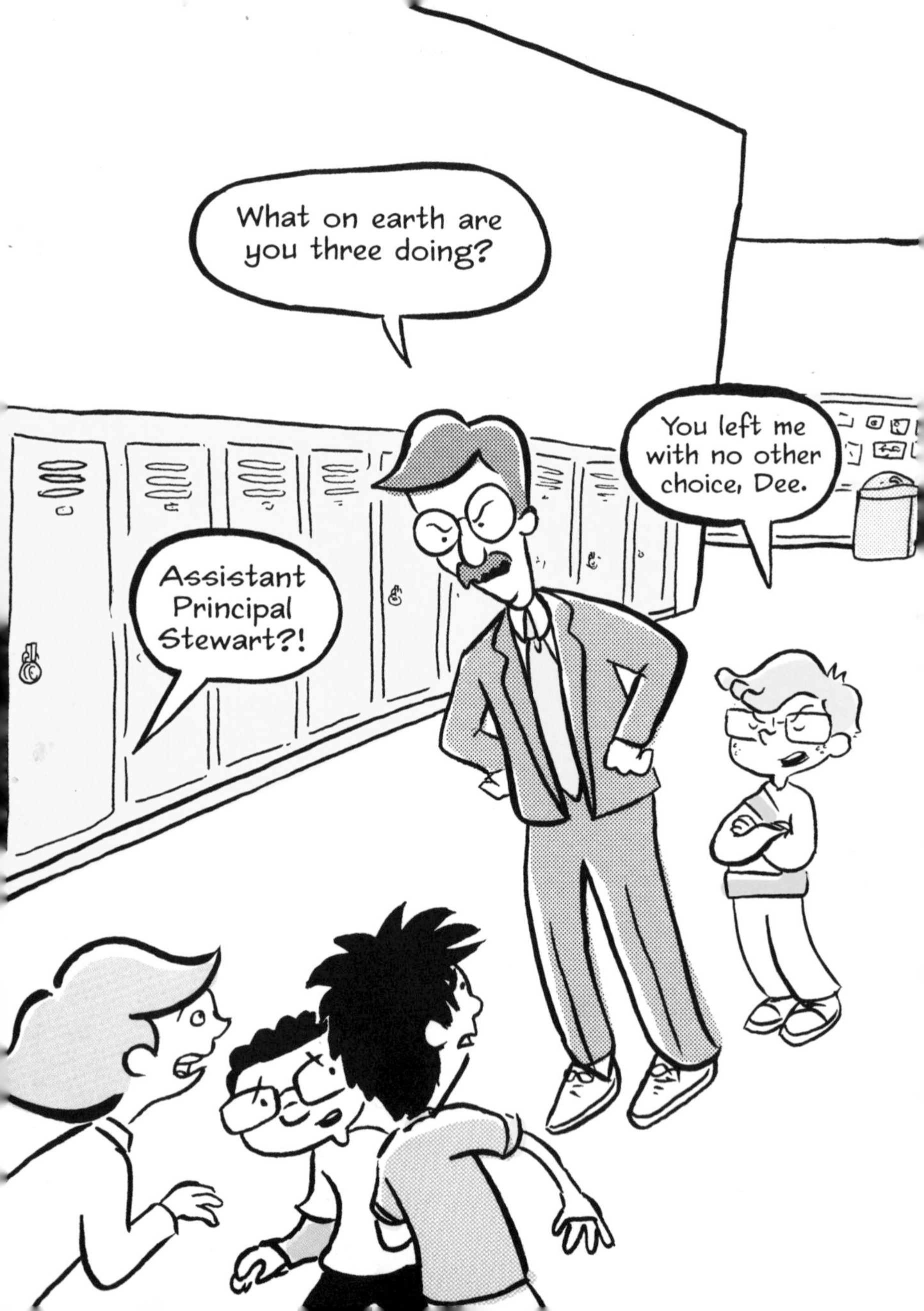
What on earth are you three doing?
Assistant Principal Stewart?!
You left me with no other choice, Dee.

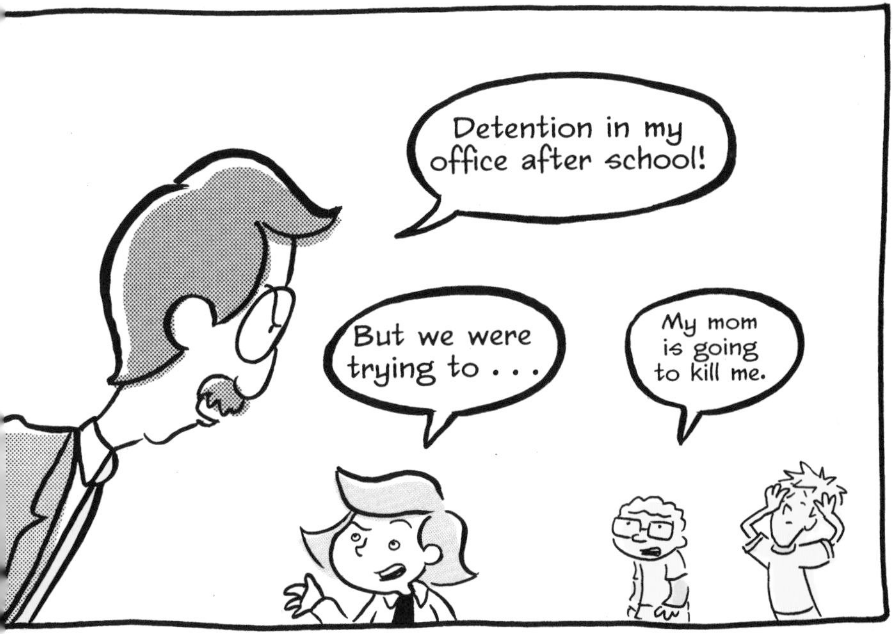
Detention in my office after school!
But we were trying to . . .
My mom is going to kill me.

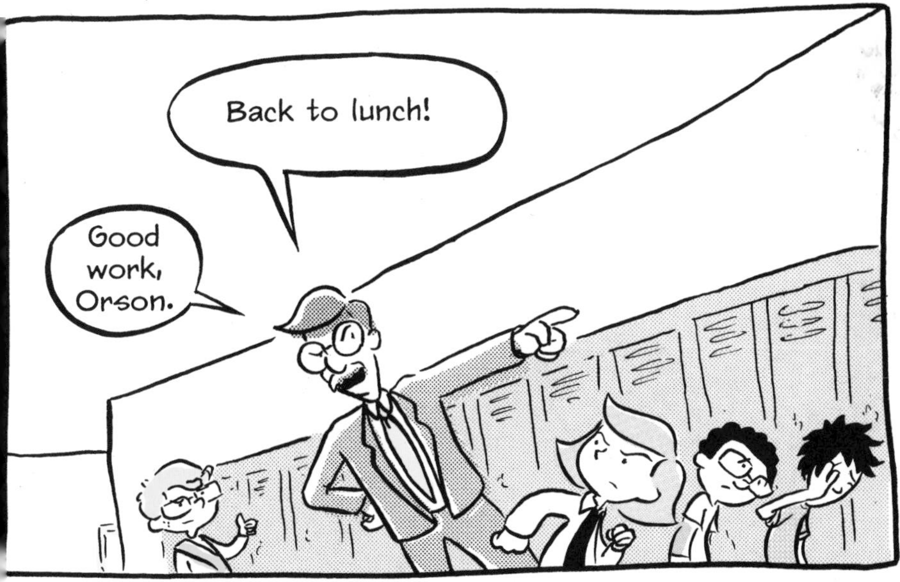
Back to lunch!
Good work, Orson.

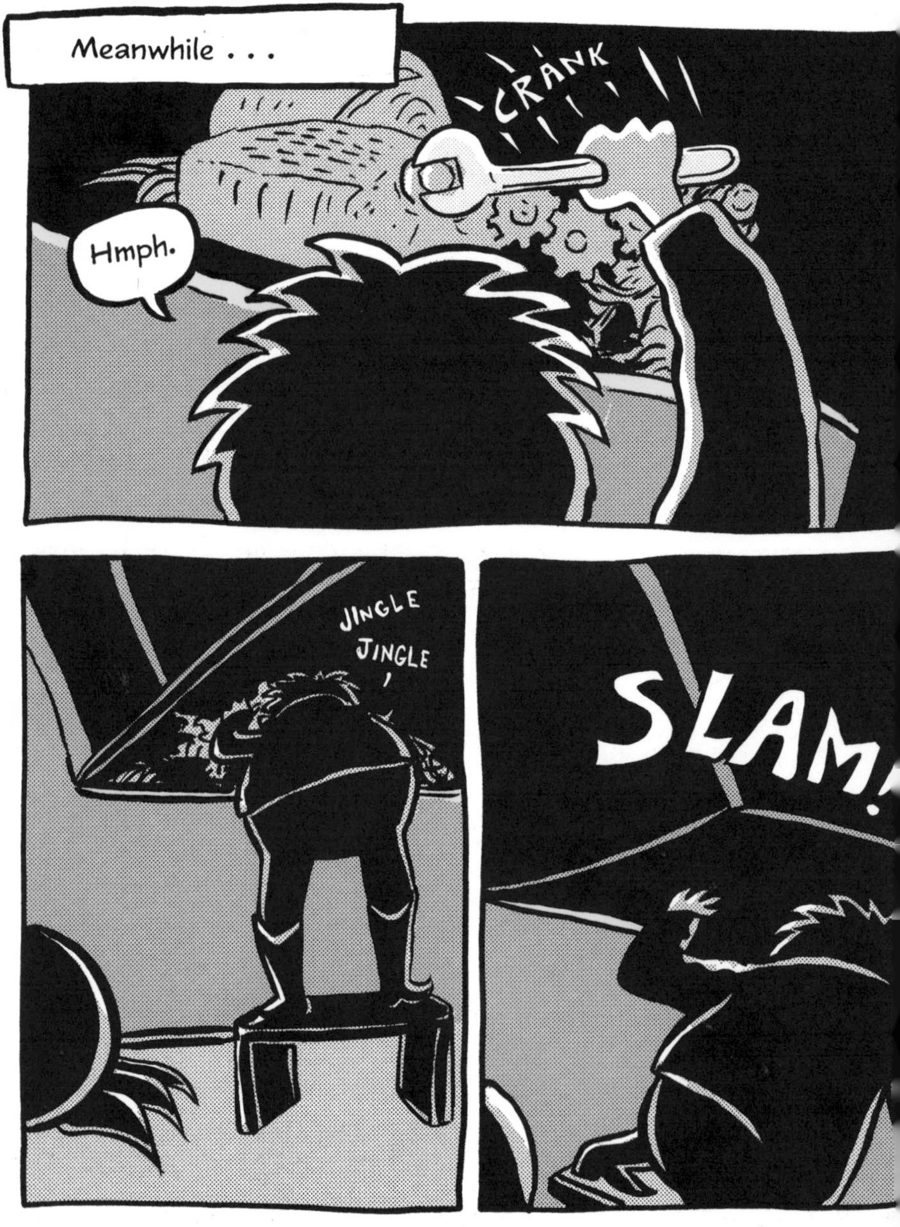
Meanwhile . . .
CRANK
Hmph.
JINGLE
JINGLE
SLAM!

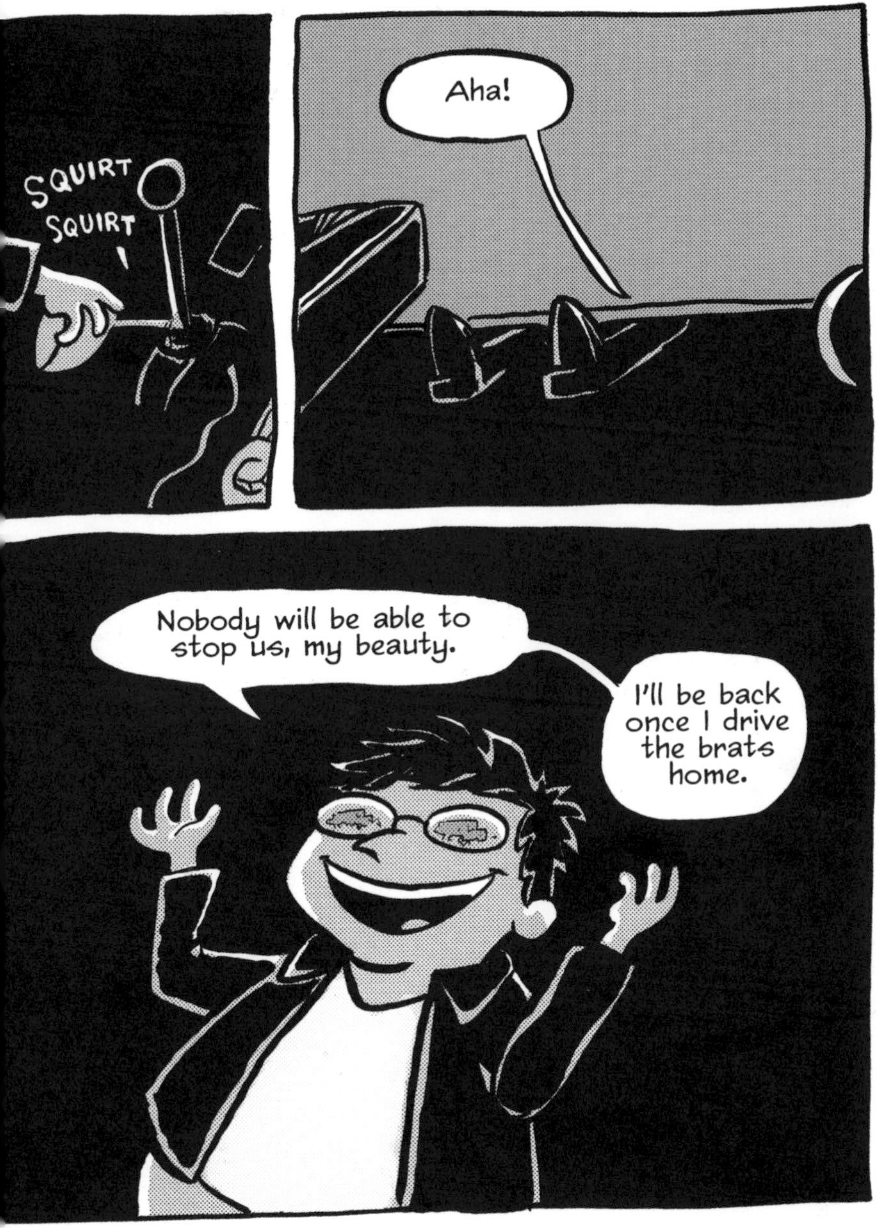
SQUIRT
SQUIRT
Aha!
Nobody will be able to stop us, my beauty.
I'll be back once I drive the brats home.

BRRRIIIII◯IIIIINNGG

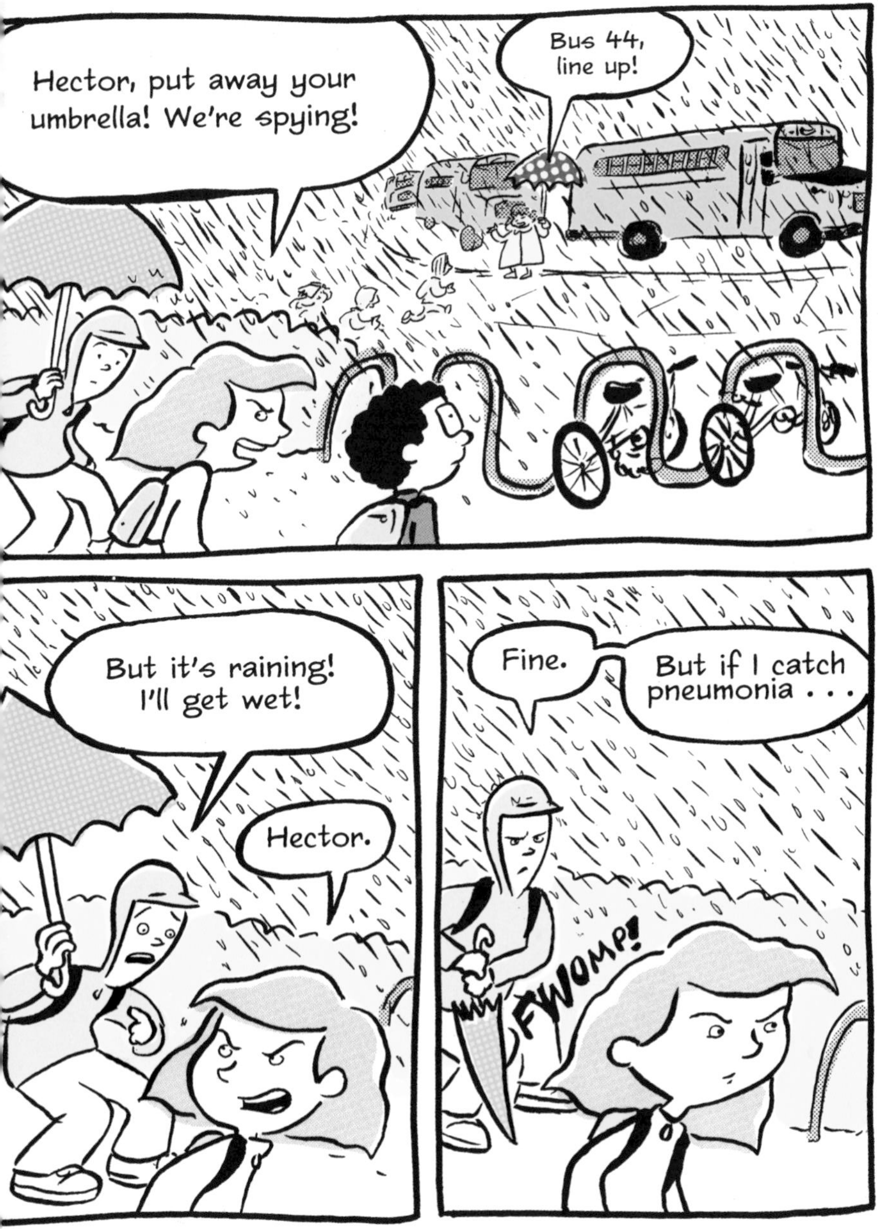
Hector, put away your umbrella! We're spying!
Bus 44, line up!
But it's raining! I'll get wet!
Hector.
Fine.
But if I catch pneumonia . . .
FWOMP!

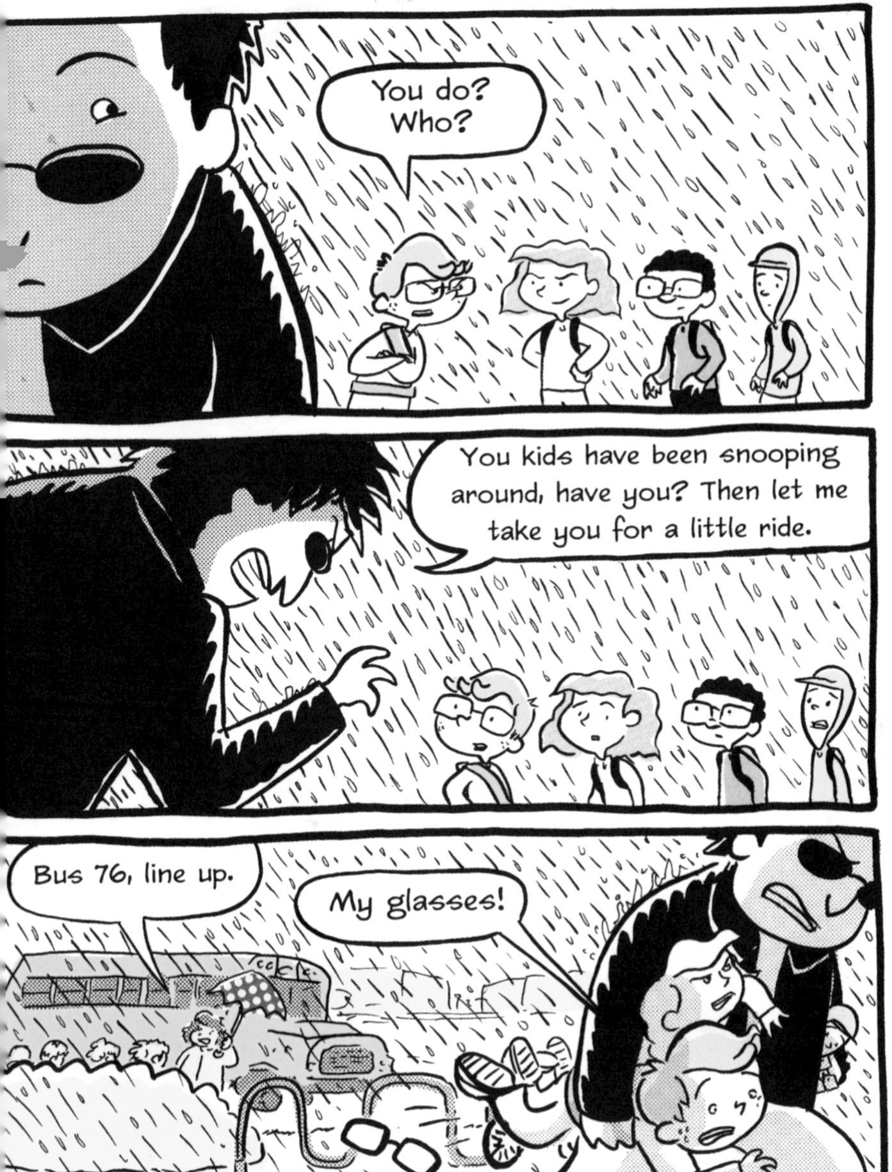
You do? Who?
You kids have been snooping around, have you? Then let me take you for a little ride.
Bus 76, line up.
My glasses!

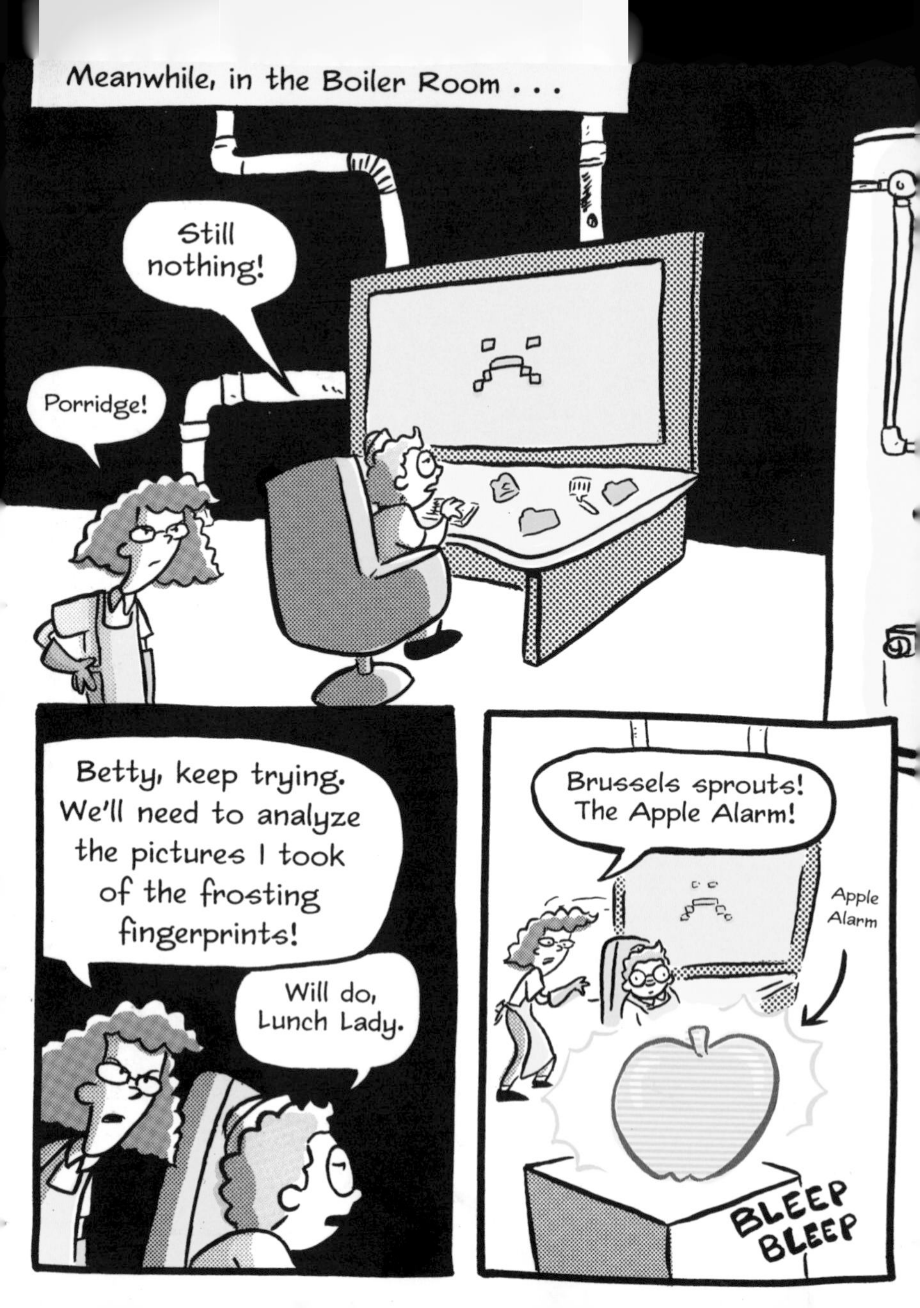

Meanwhile, in the Boiler Room . . .
Still nothing!
Porridge!
Betty, keep trying. We'll need to analyze the pictures I took of the frosting fingerprints!
Will do, Lunch Lady.
Brussels sprouts! The Apple Alarm!
Apple Alarm
BLEEP BLEEP

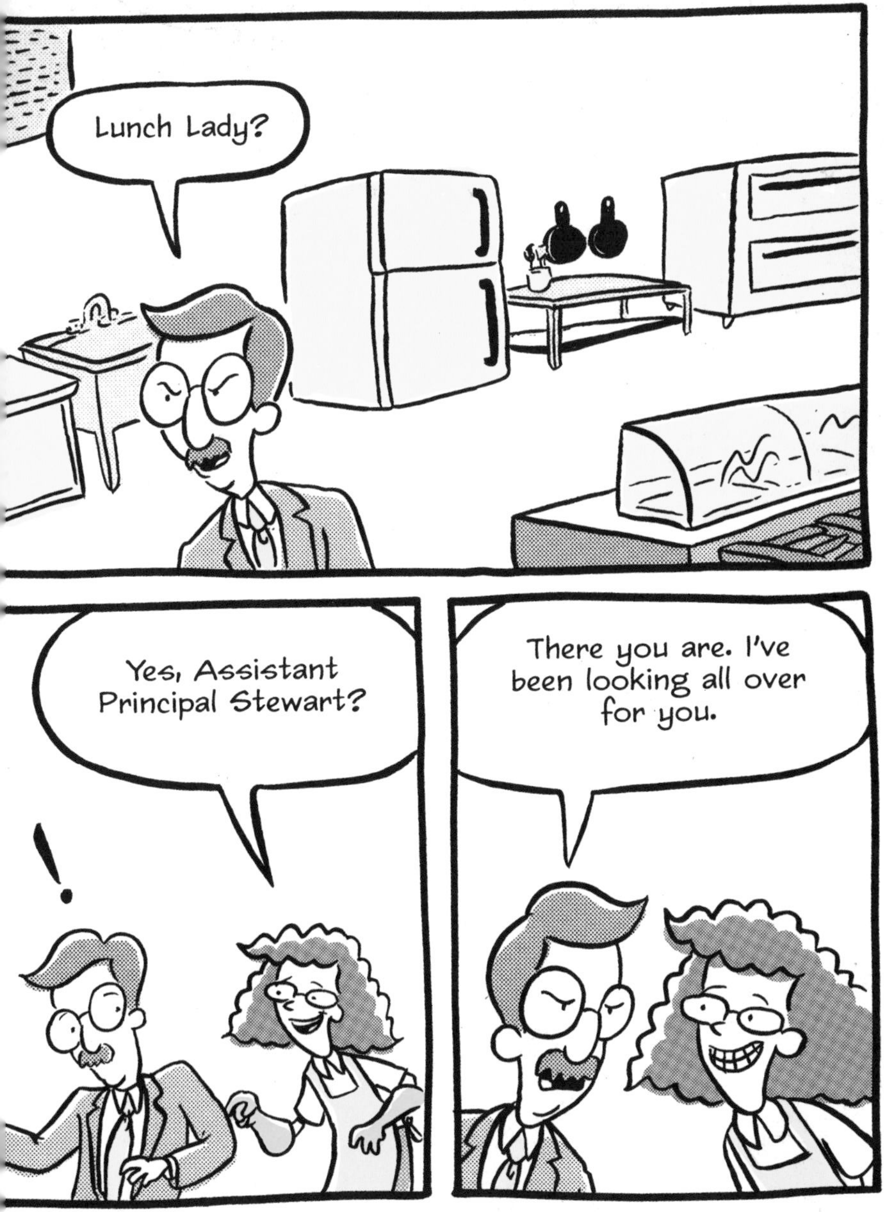
Lunch Lady?
Yes, Assistant Principal Stewart?
!
There you are. I've been looking all over for you.

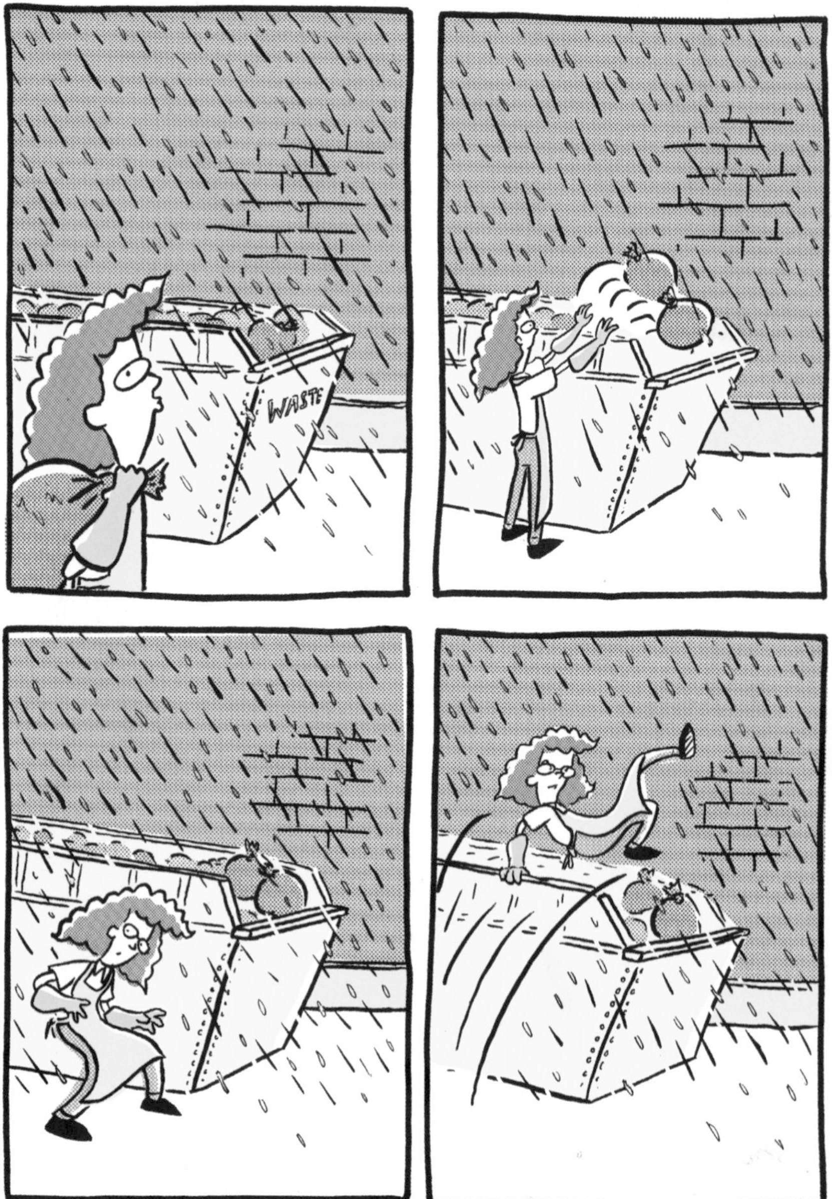
WASTE

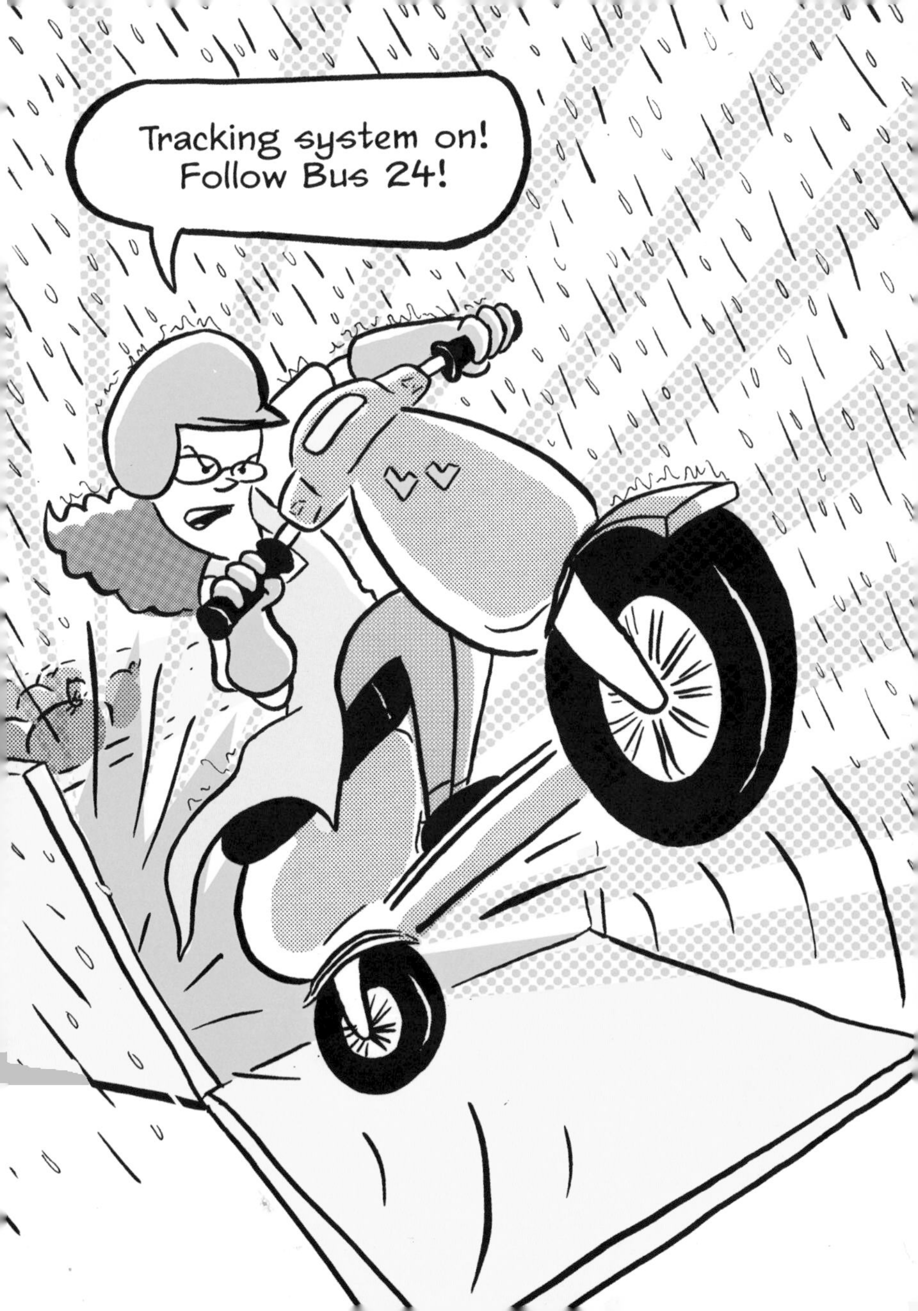
Tracking system on! Follow Bus 24!

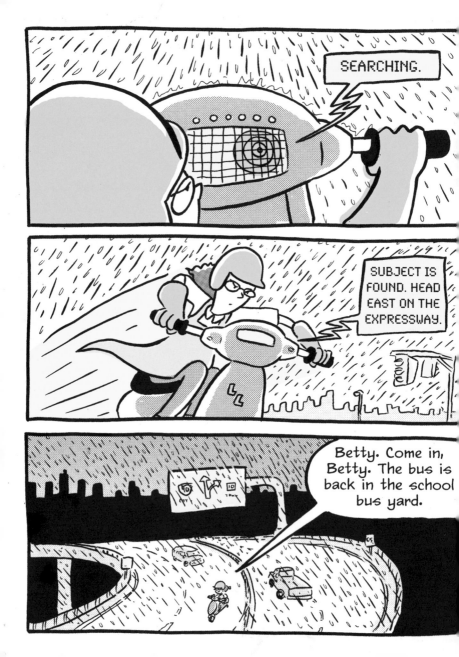

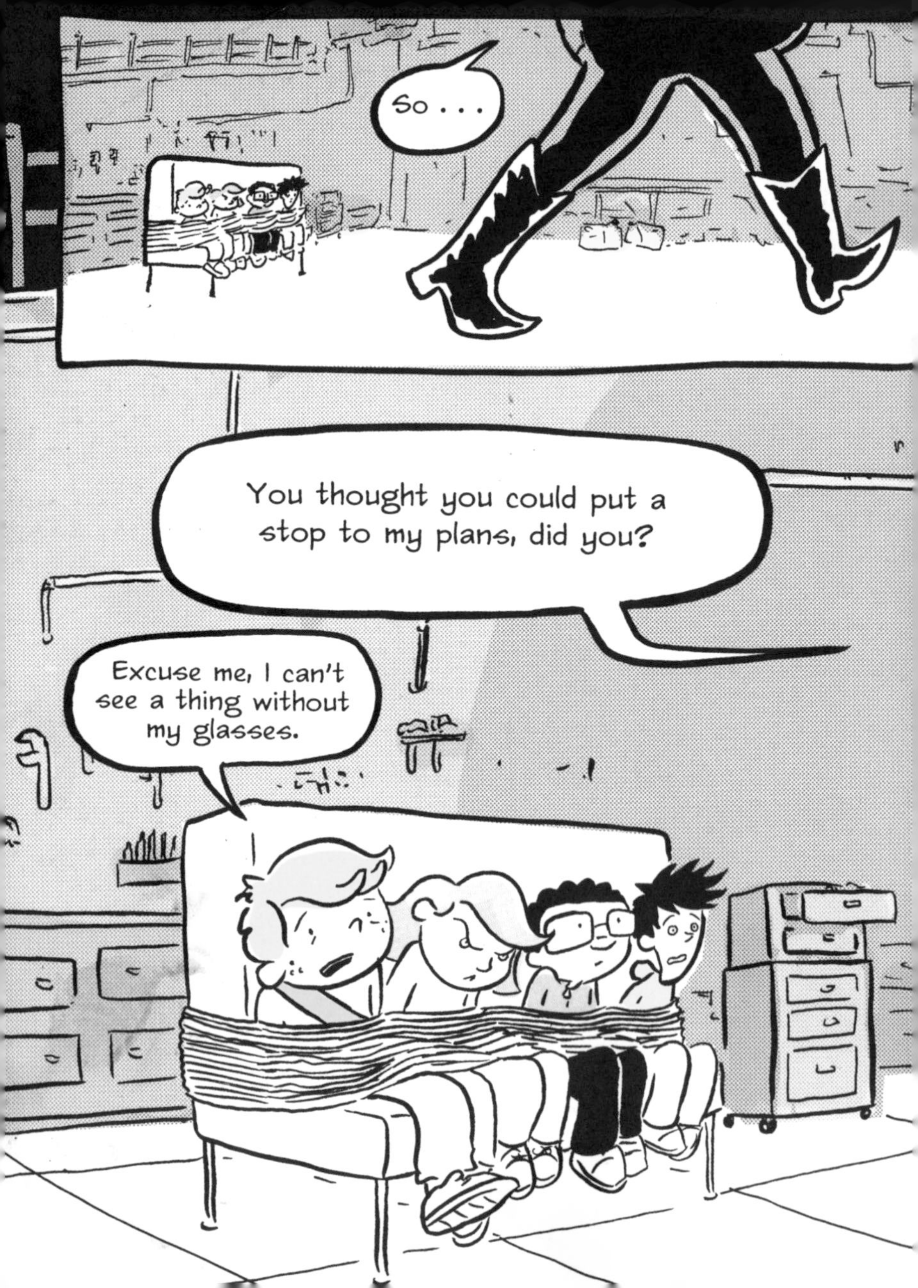
So . . .
You thought you could put a stop to my plans, did you?
Excuse me, I can't see a thing without my glasses.

Betty, I'm atop the garage in the school bus yard!
Now to find bus driver Brenda.
I'm on my way!

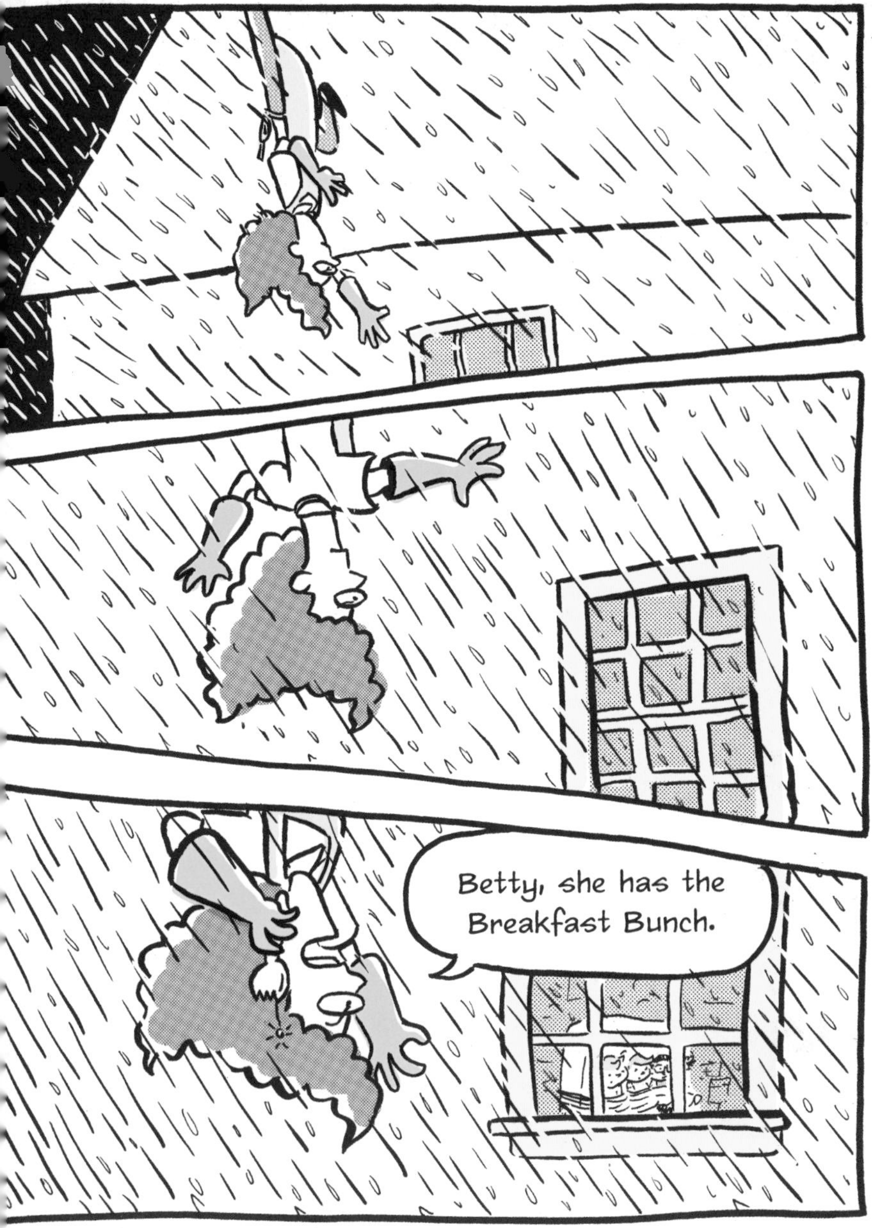
Betty, she has the Breakfast Bunch.

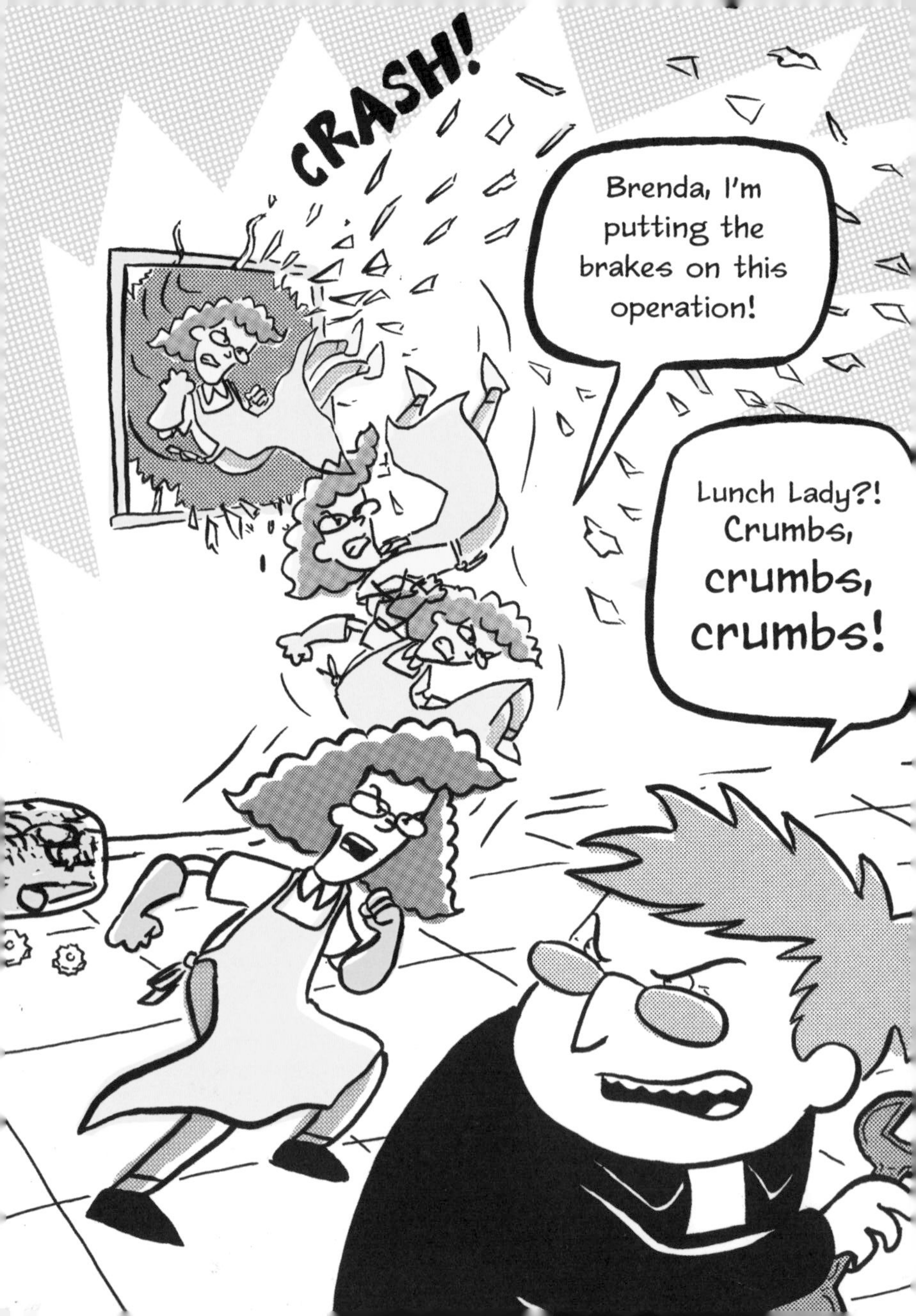
CRASH!
Brenda, I'm putting the brakes on this operation!
Lunch Lady?! Crumbs, crumbs, crumbs!

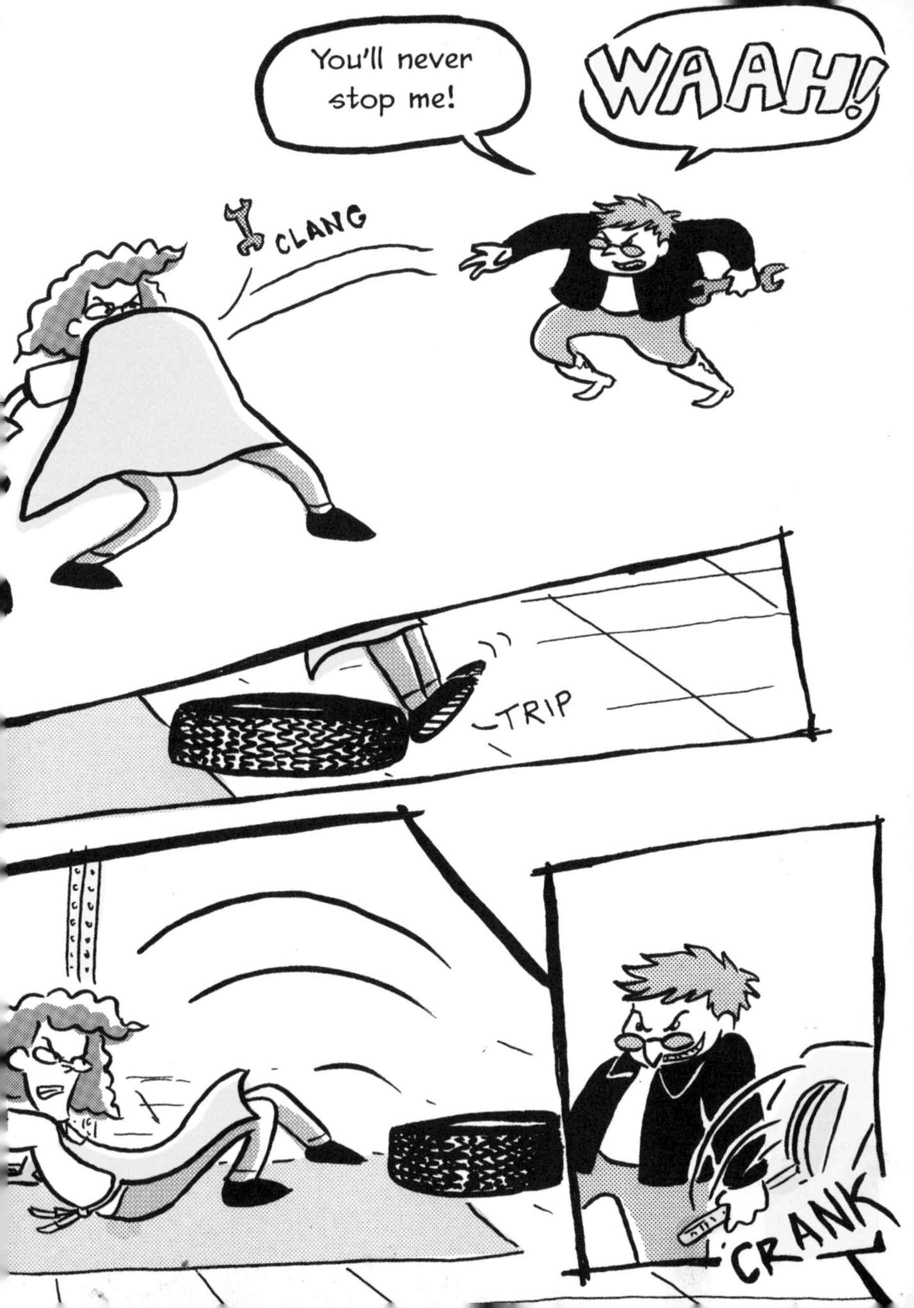
You'll never stop me!
WAAH!
CLANG
TRIP
CRANK

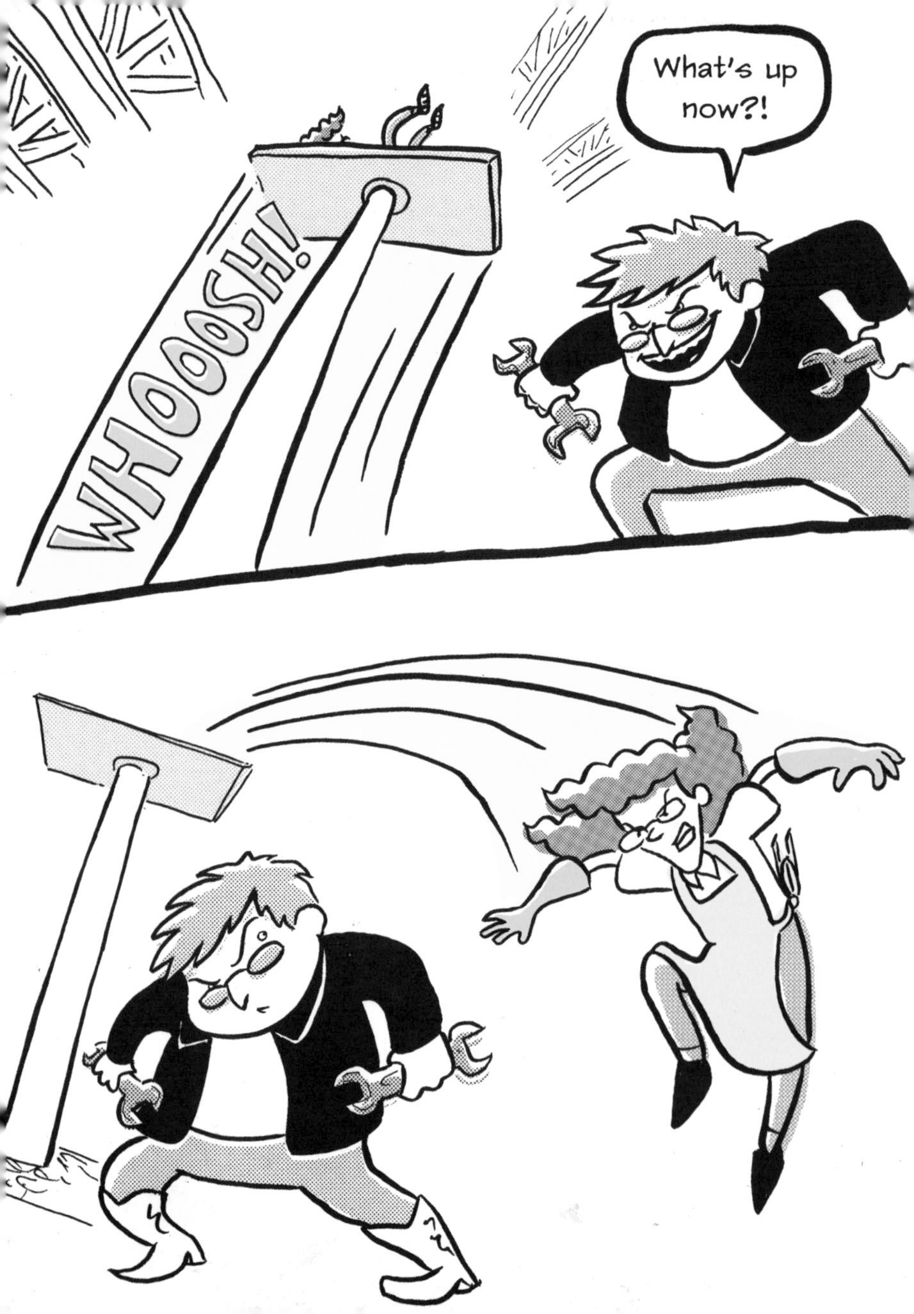
WHOOOSH!
What's up now?!

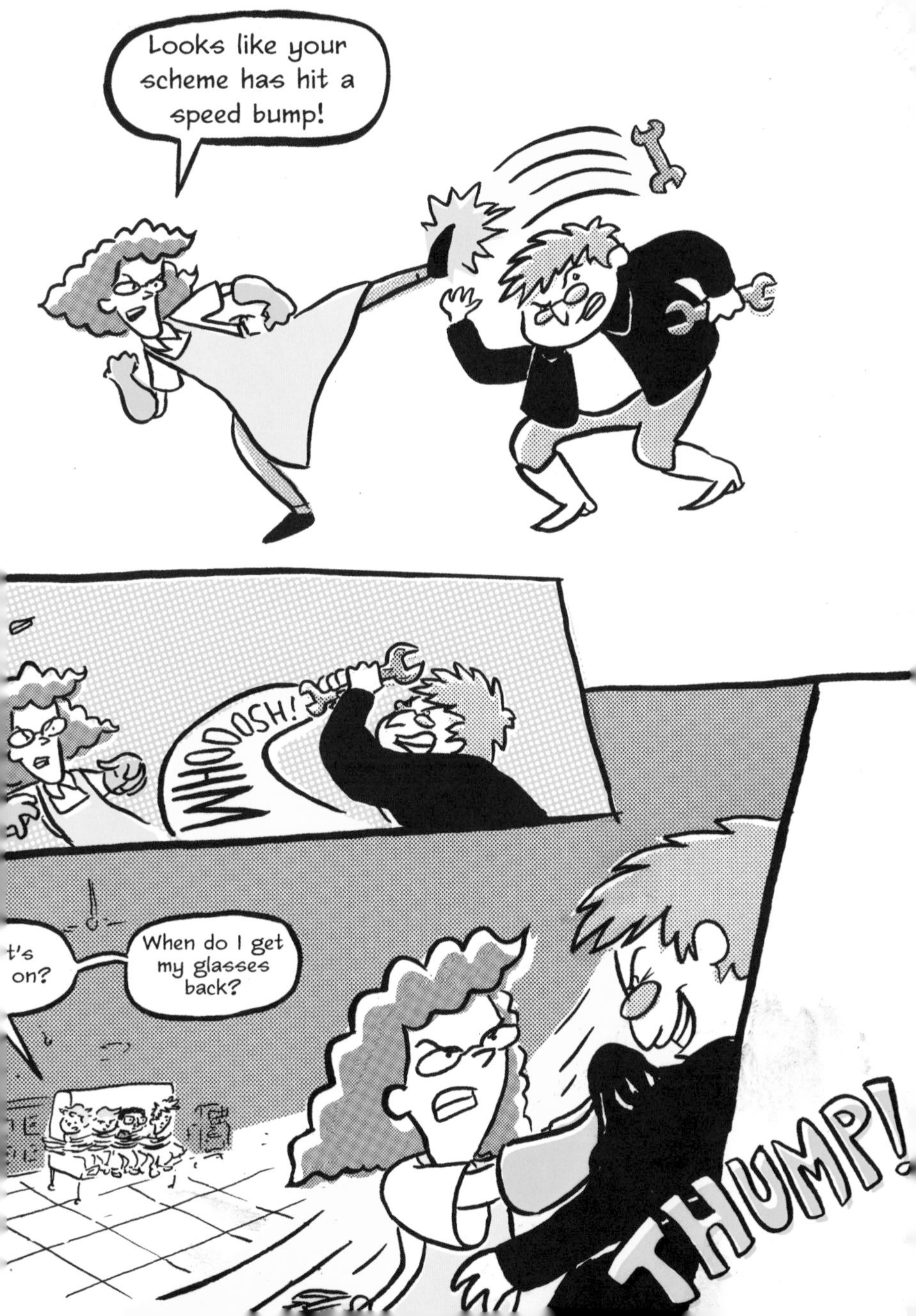
Looks like your scheme has hit a speed bump!
WHOOOOSH!
When do I get my glasses back?
THUMP!

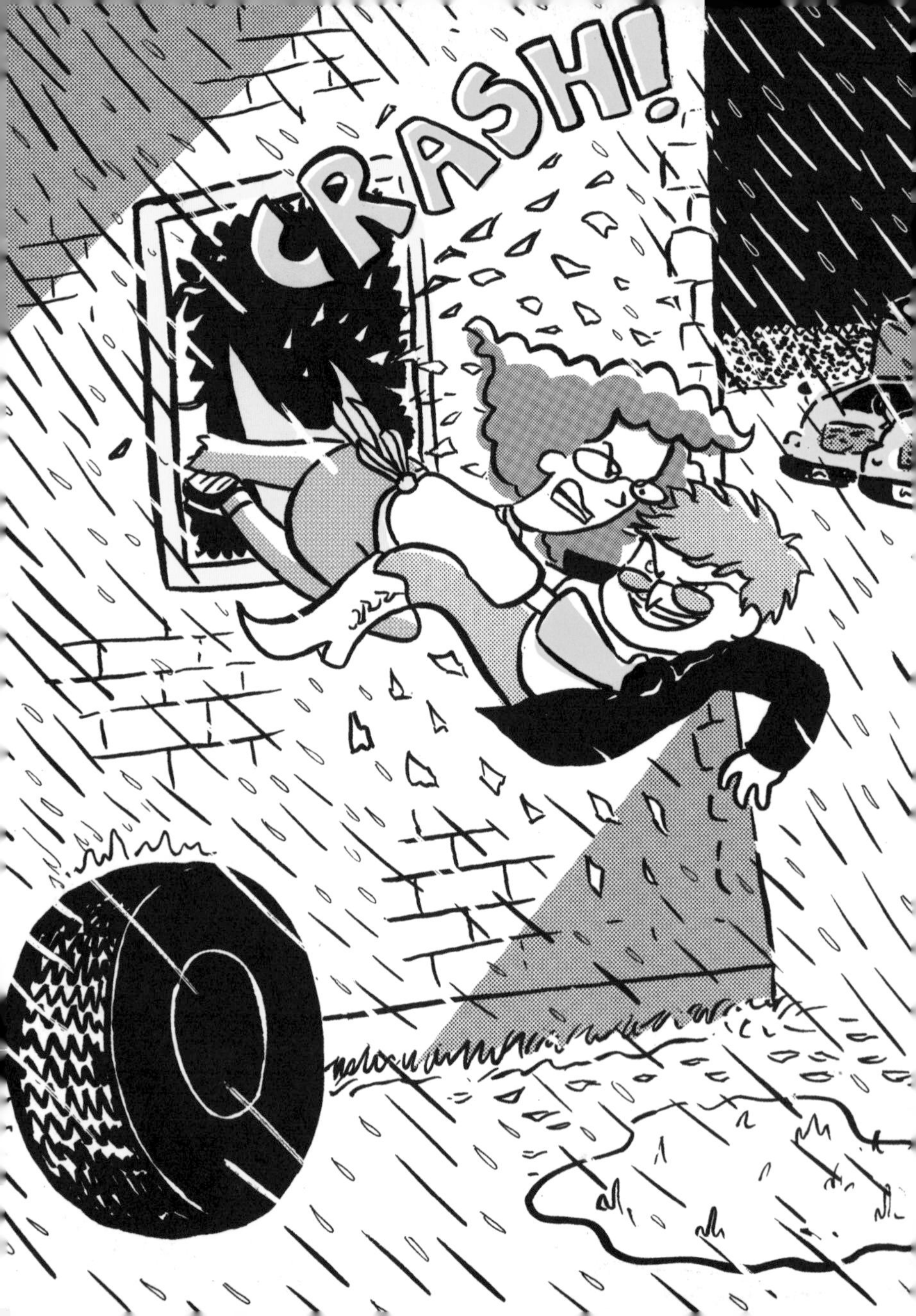
CRASH!

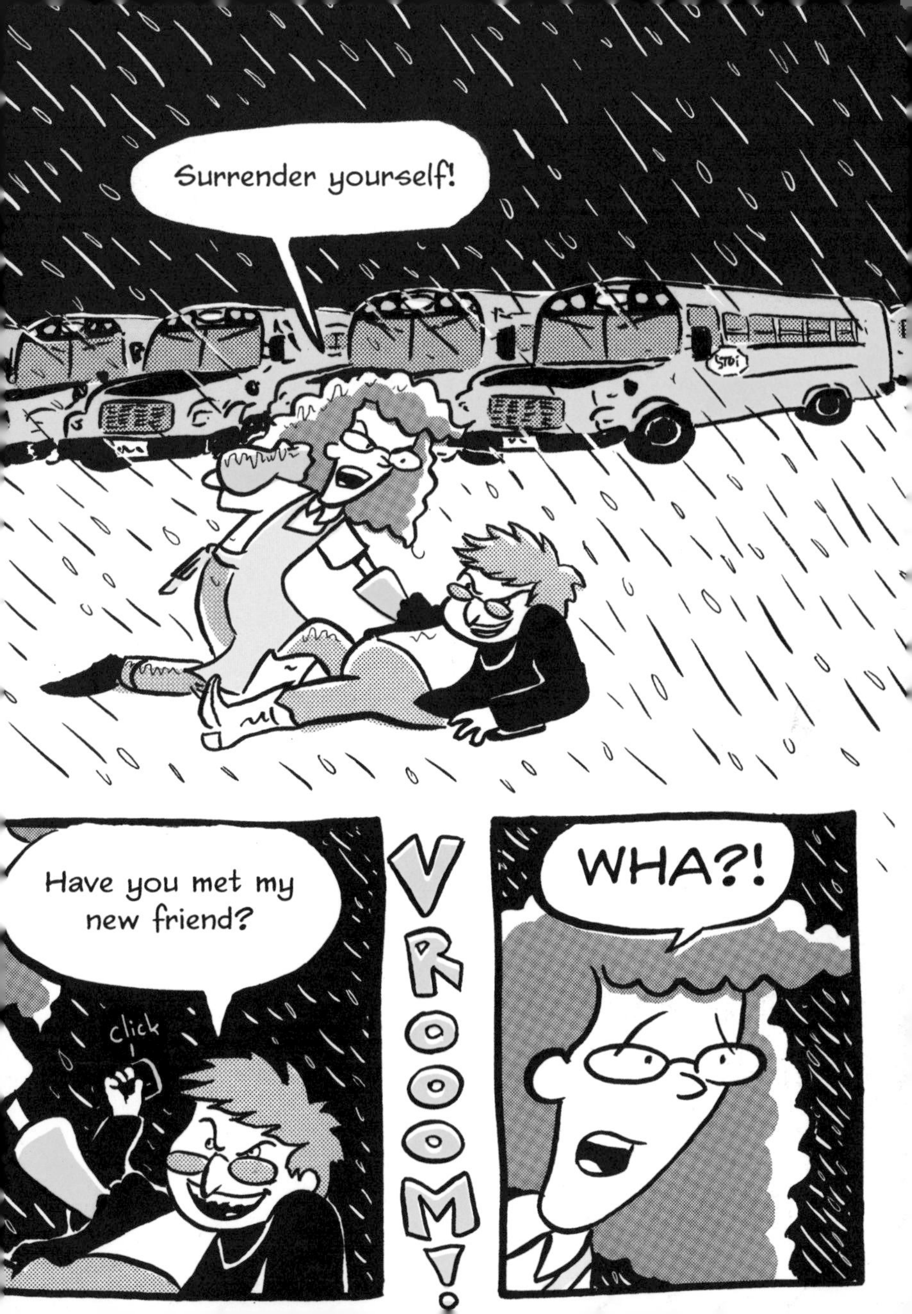
Surrender yourself!
Have you met my new friend?
click
VROOOOM!
WHA?!

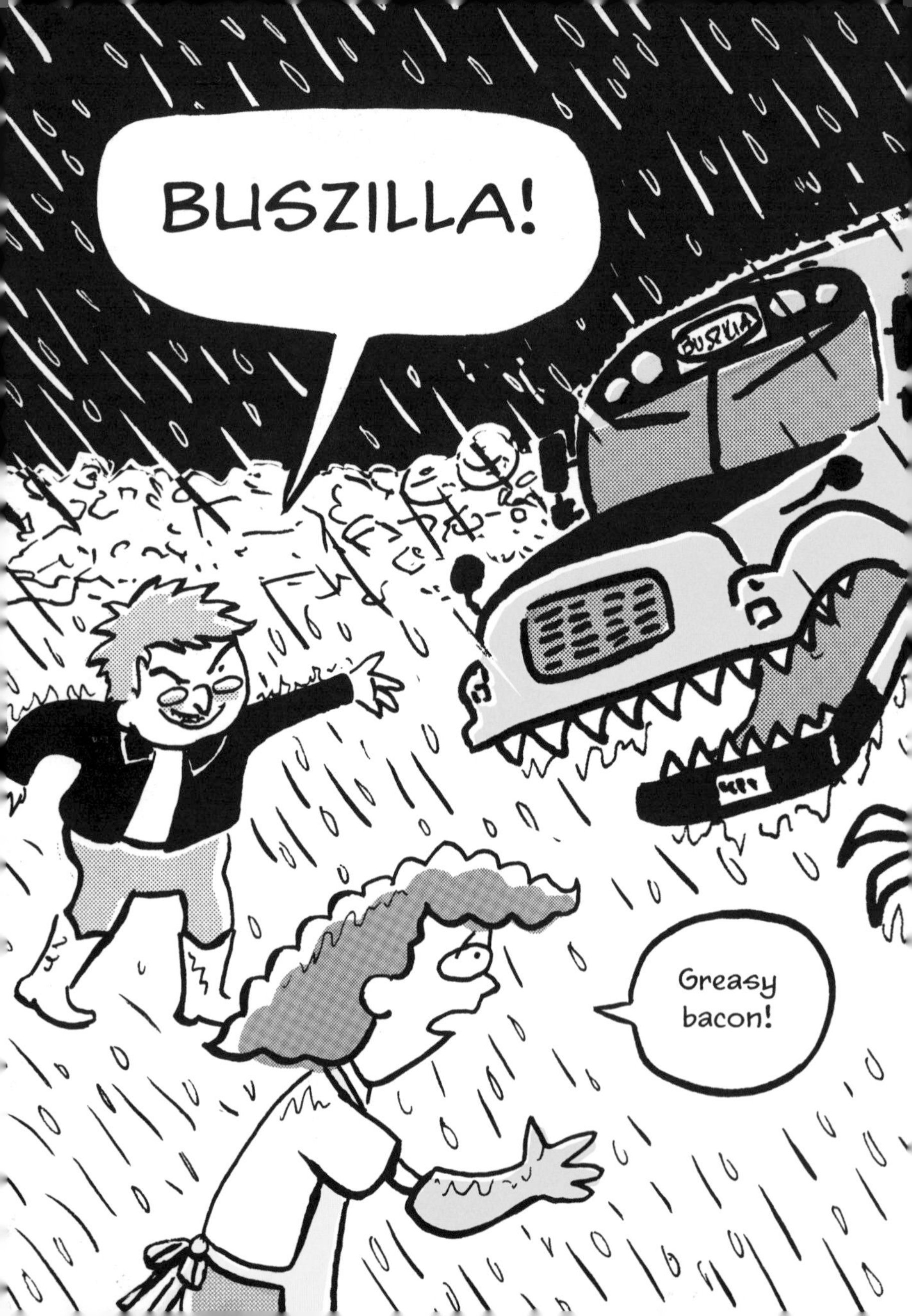
BUSZILLA!
Greasy bacon!

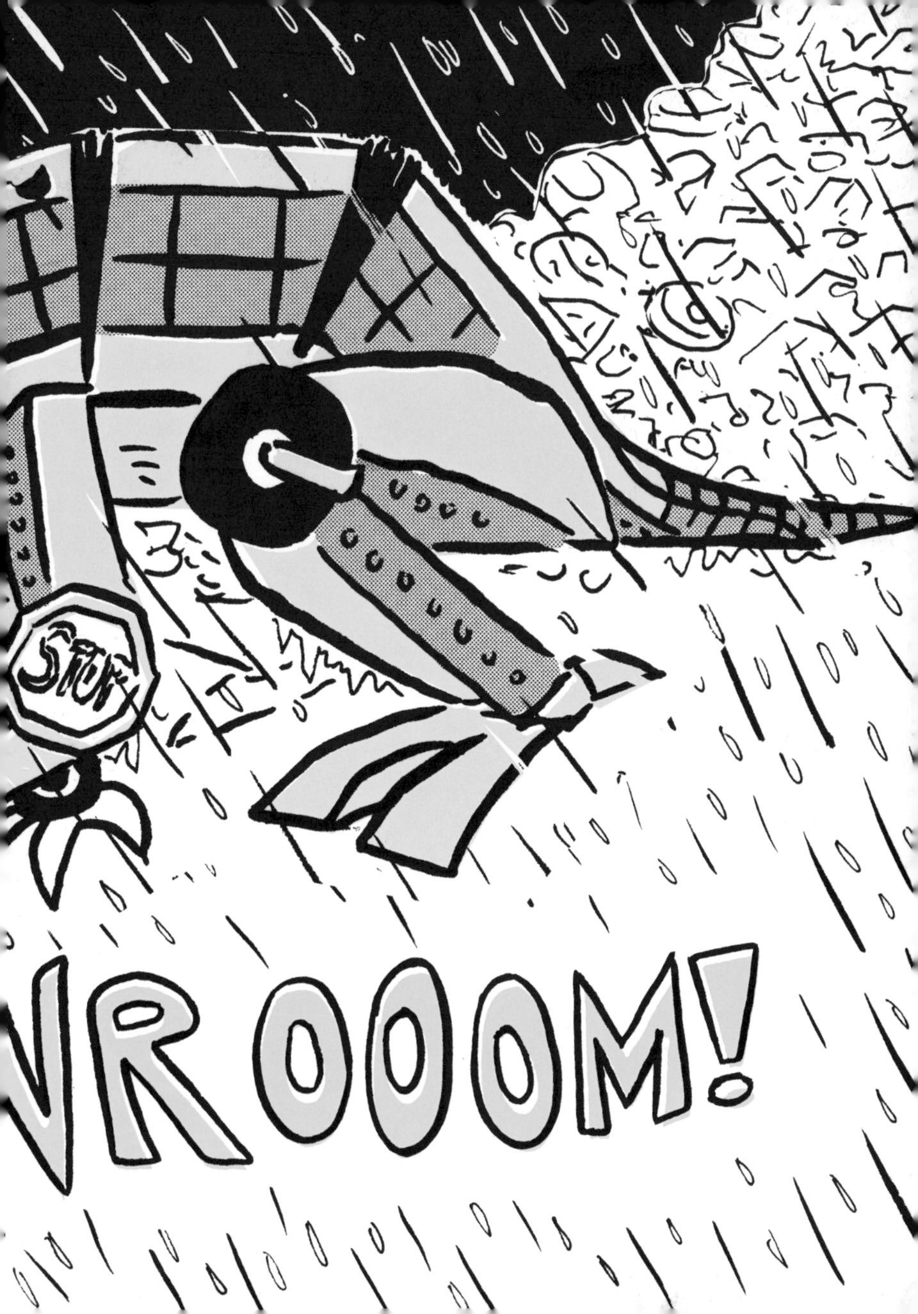
VROOOM!

Oooh, it feels good to get behind the wheel!
STOP
turn
VROOM
VROOM!
CRANK

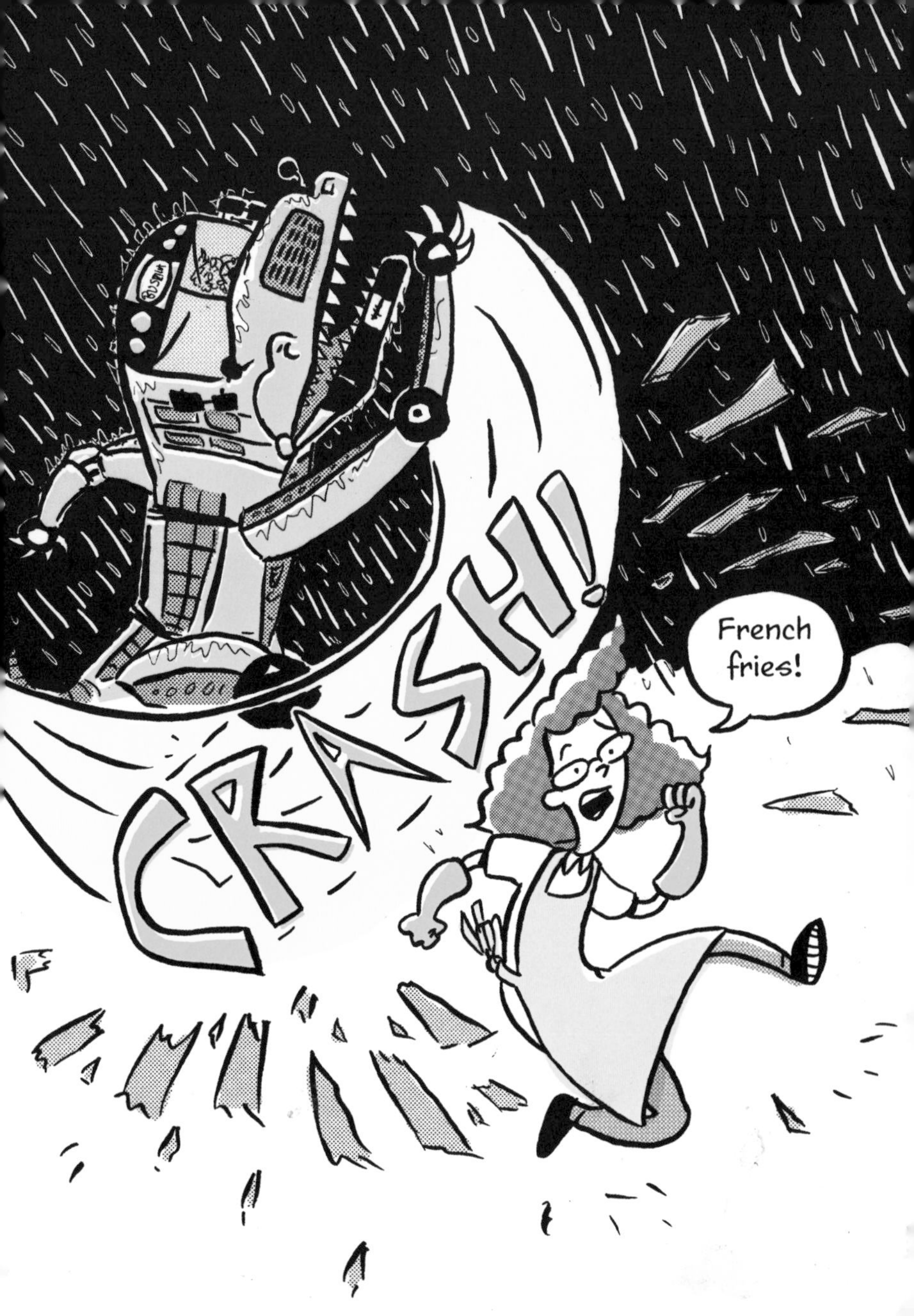
CRASH!!
French fries!

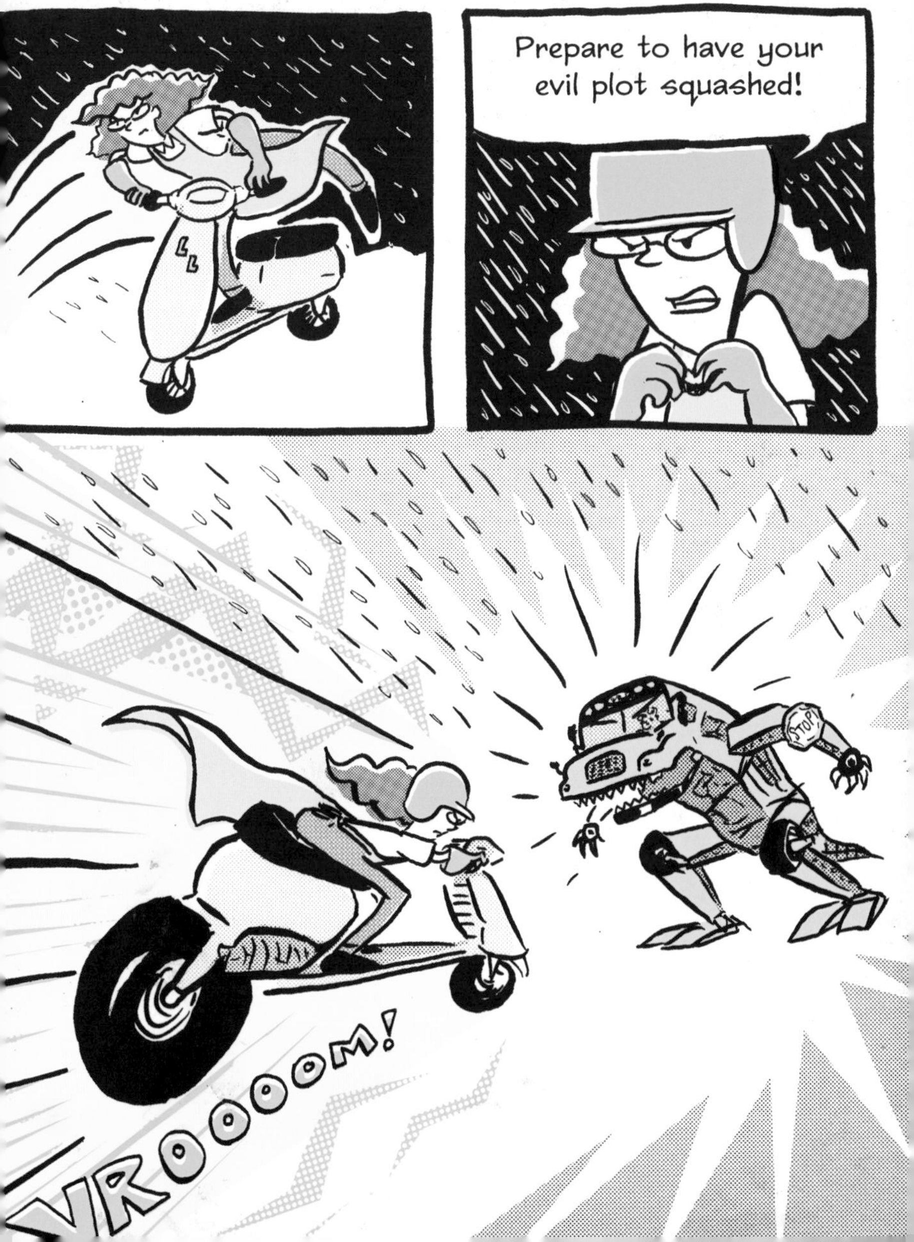
Prepare to have your evil plot squashed!
STOP
VROOOOOM!

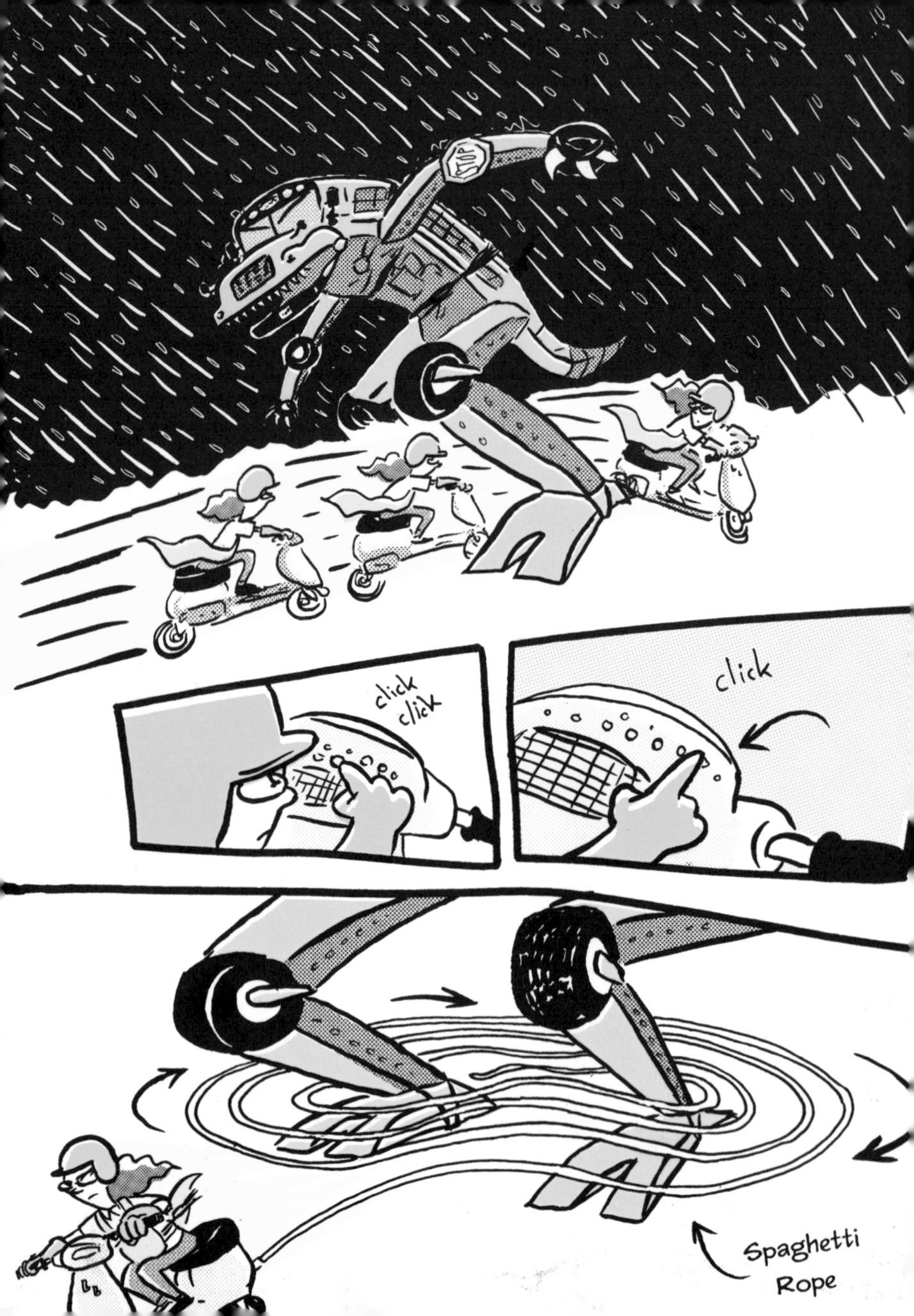
STOP
click
click
click
Spaghetti
Rope
LB

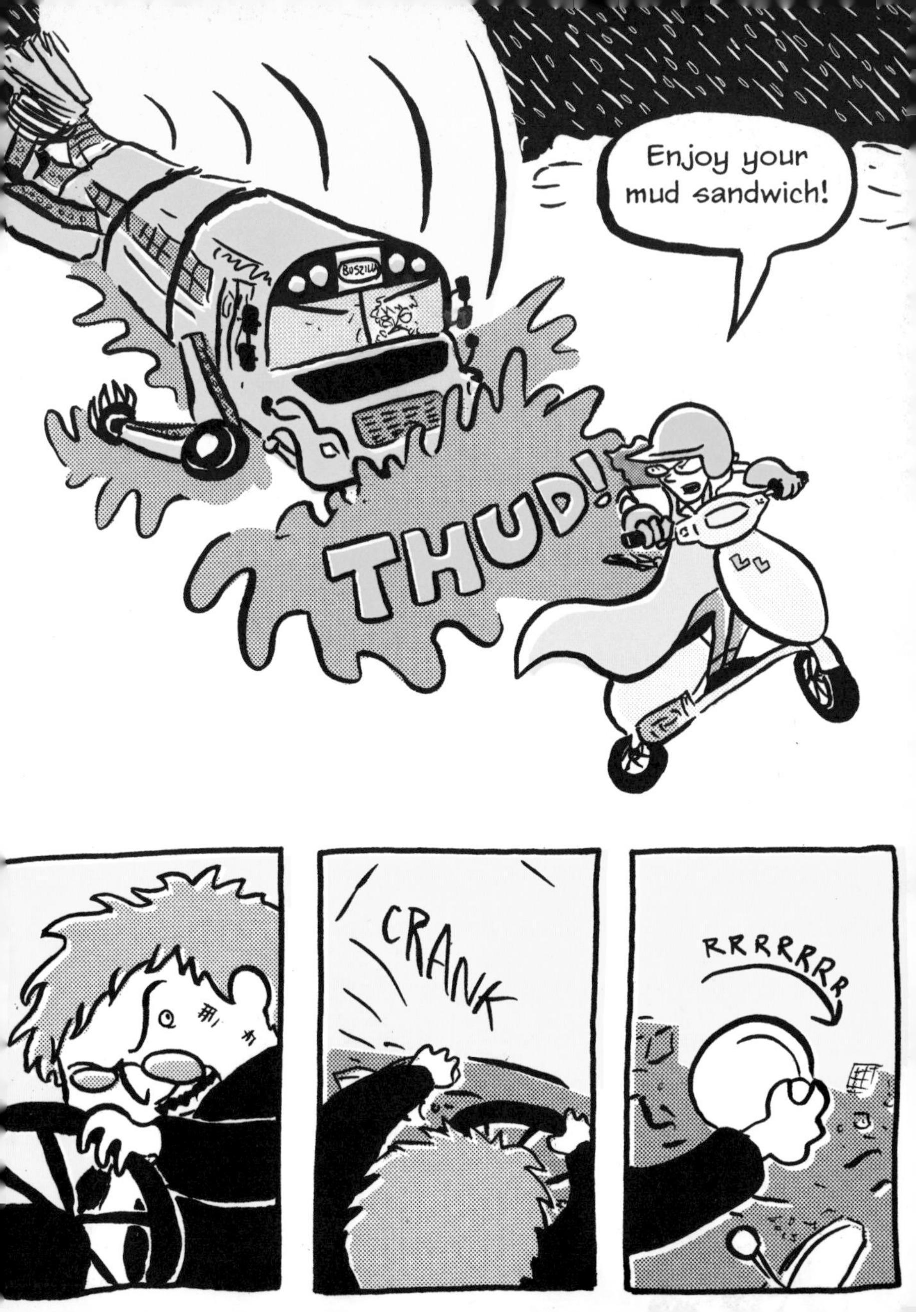
Enjoy your mud sandwich!
THUD!
CRANK
RRRRRRRR

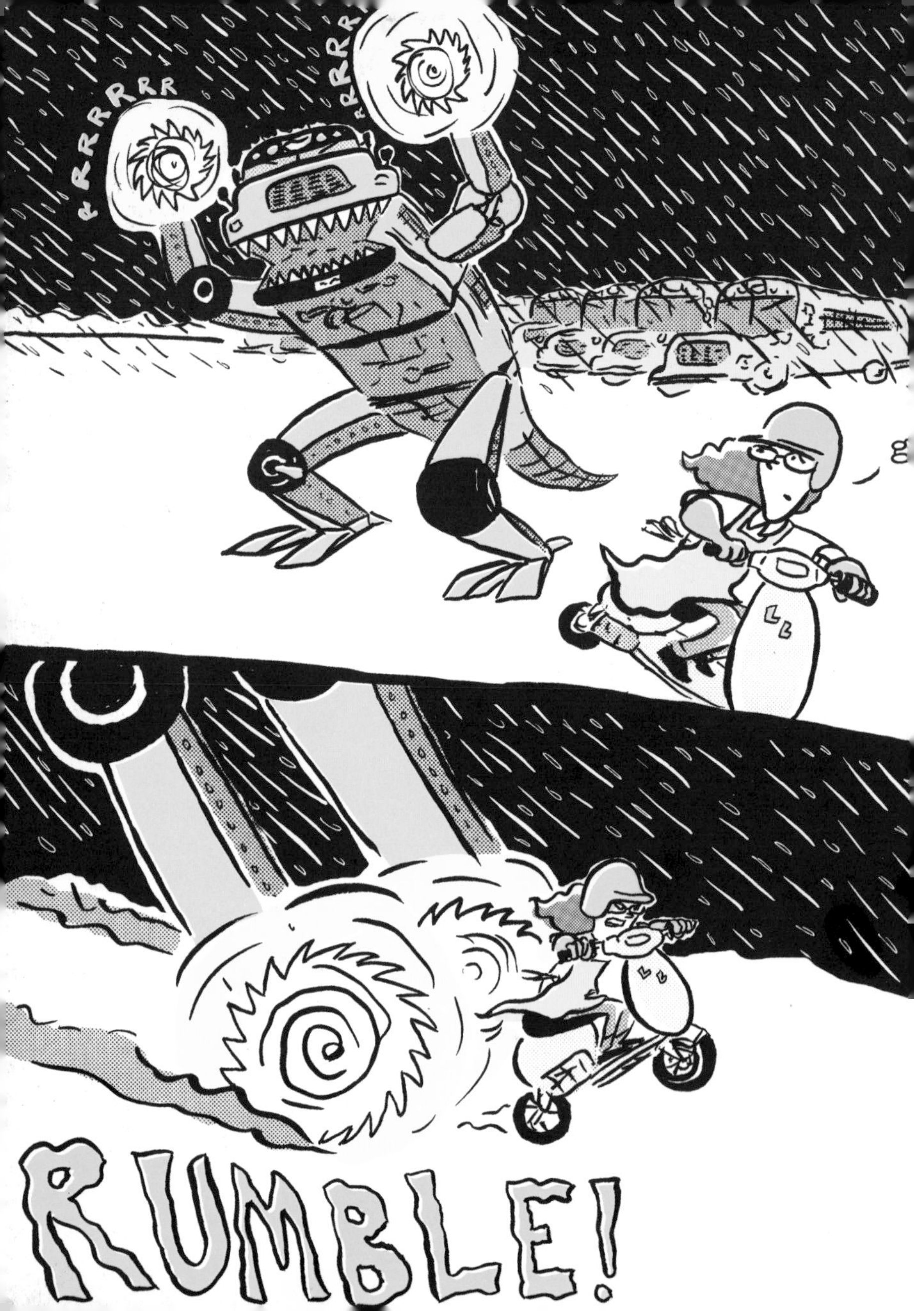

RRRRRRR
RRRRR
g
RUMBLE!

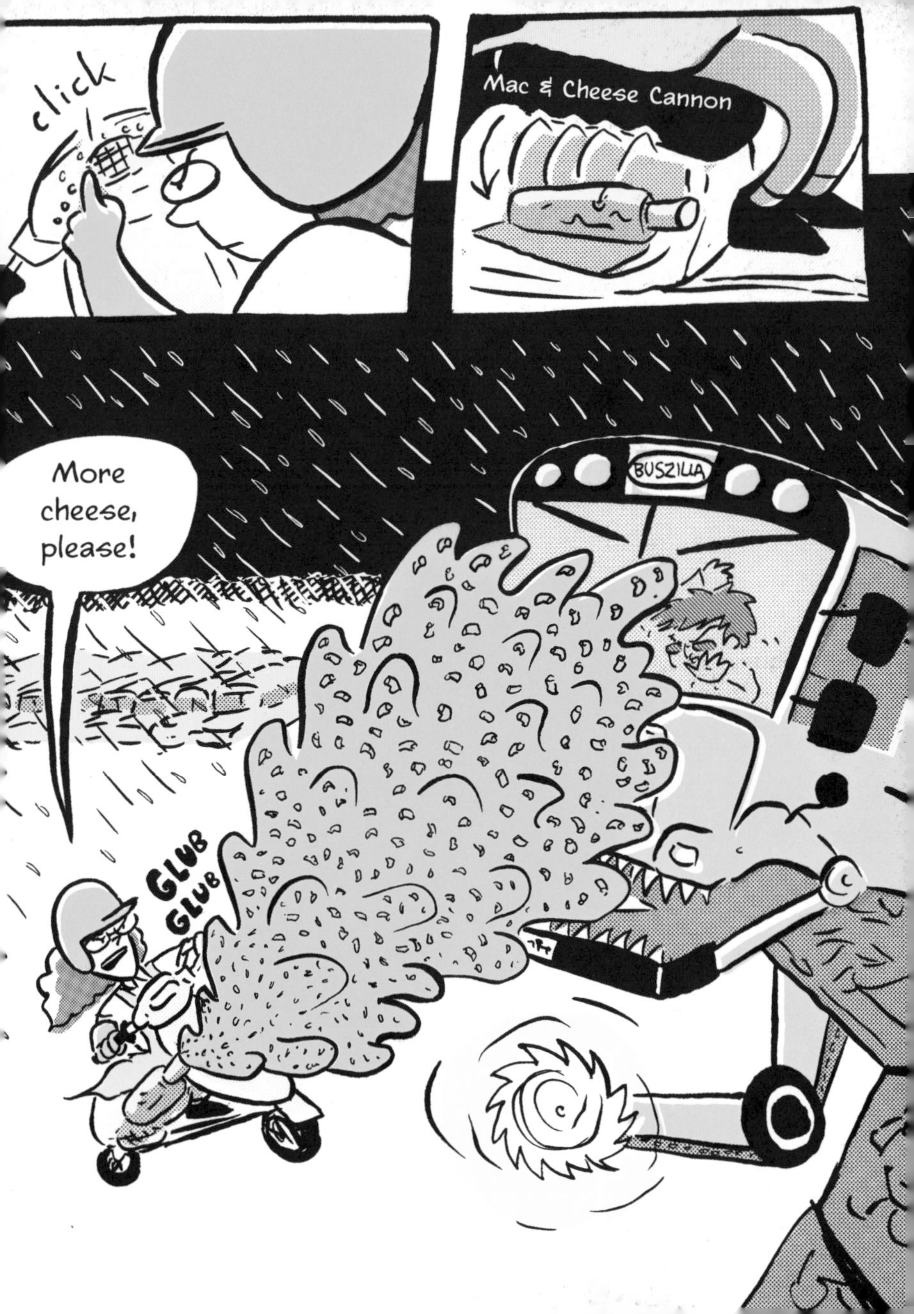
click
Mac & Cheese Cannon
BUSZILLA
More cheese, please!
GLUB GLUB

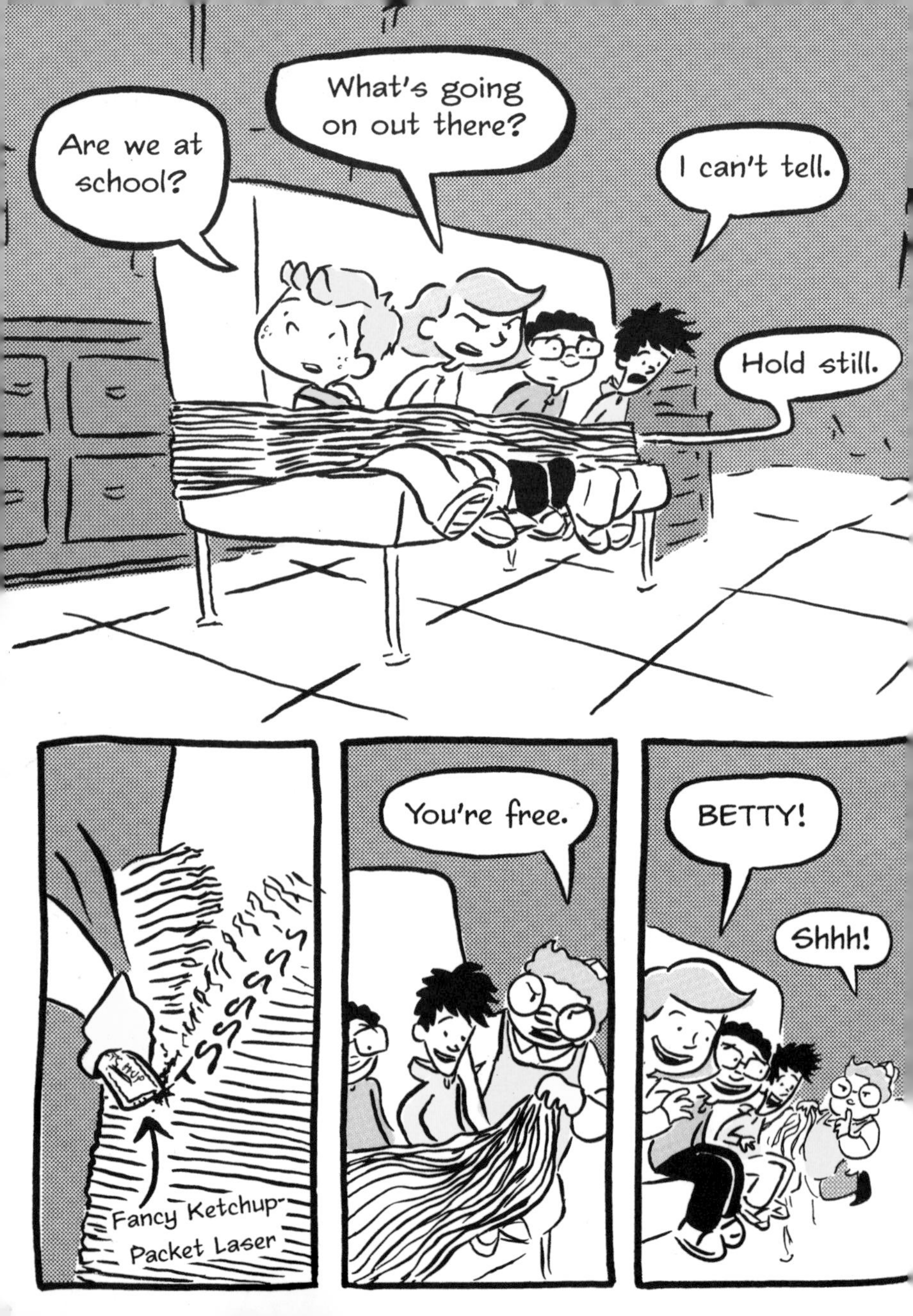
Are we at school?
What's going on out there?
I can't tell.
Hold still.
Fancy Ketchup Packet Laser
TSSSSSSS
You're free.
BETTY!
Shhh!

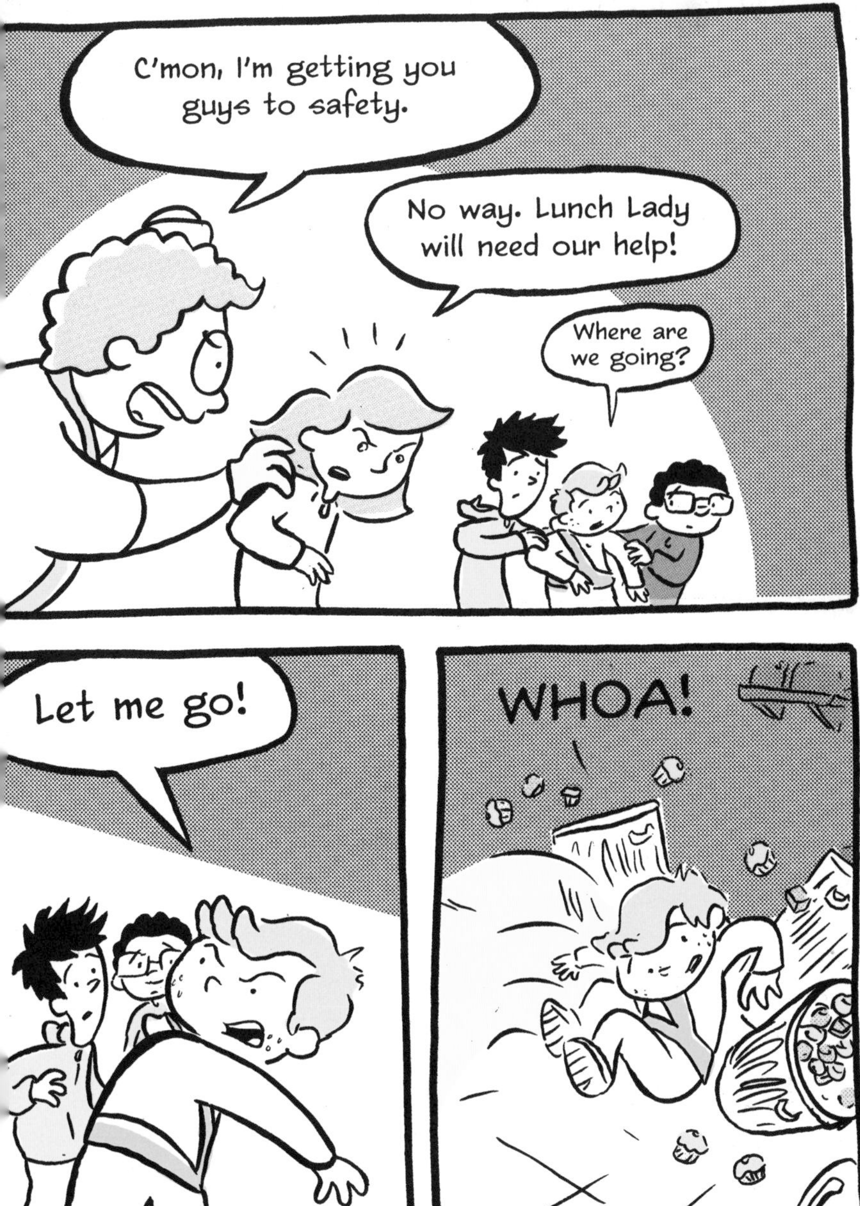
C'mon, I'm getting you guys to safety.
No way. Lunch Lady will need our help!
Where are we going?
Let me go!
WHOA!

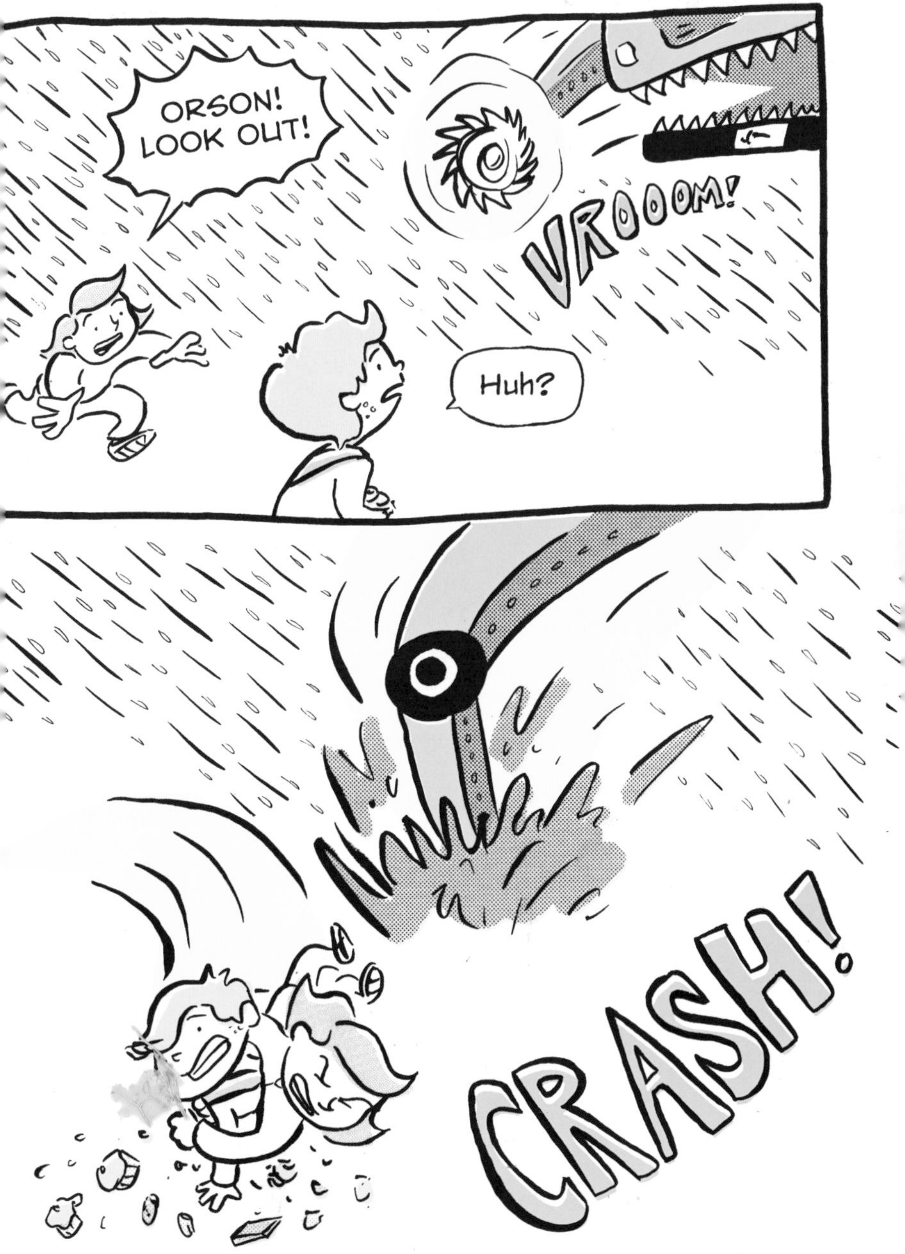
ORSON! LOOK OUT!
VROOOM!
Huh?
CRASH!

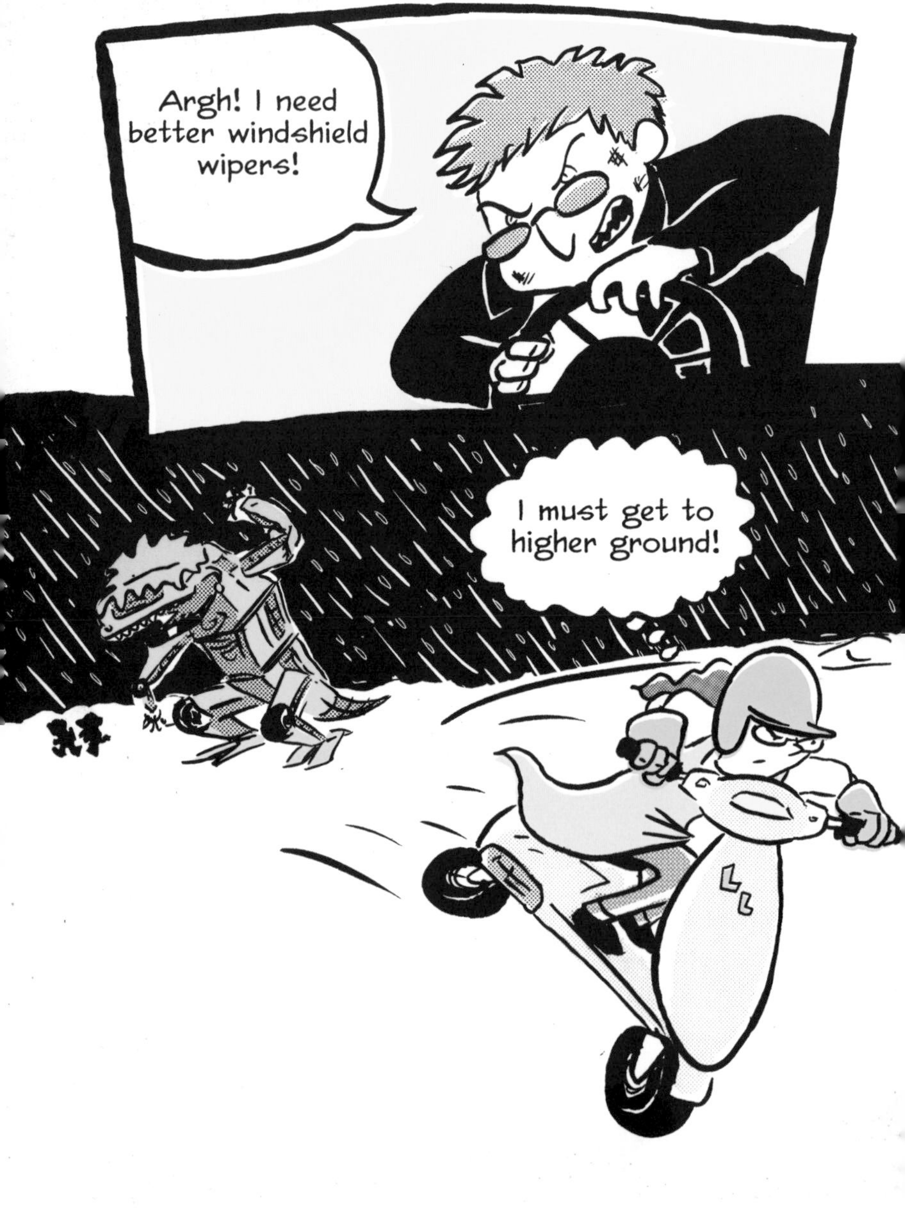
Argh! I need better windshield wipers!
I must get to higher ground!

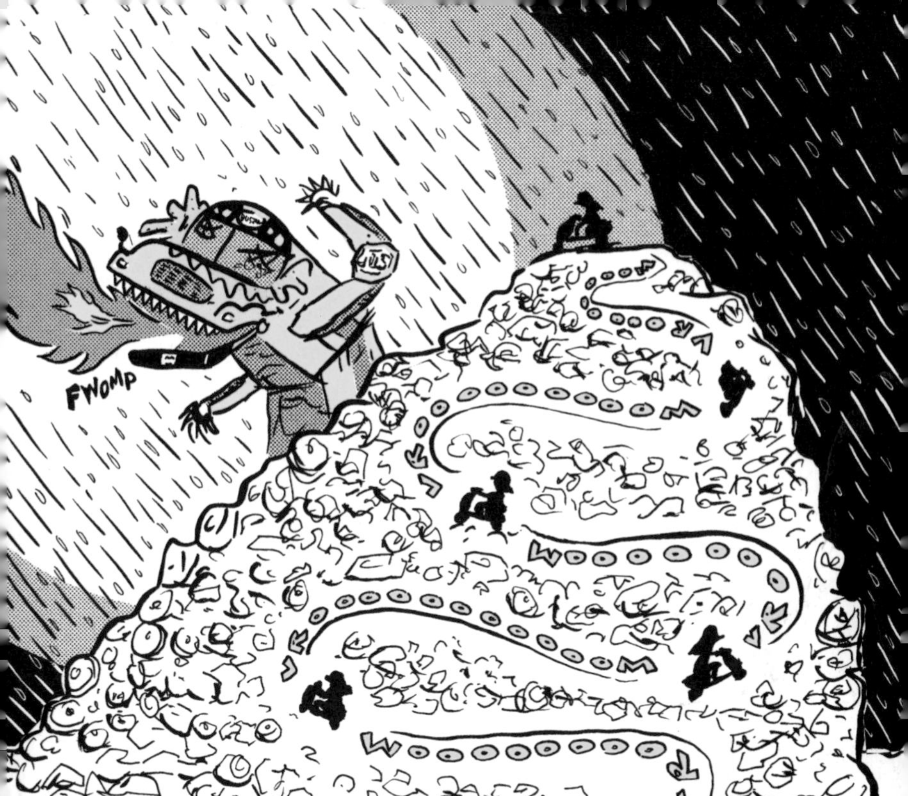
FWOMP

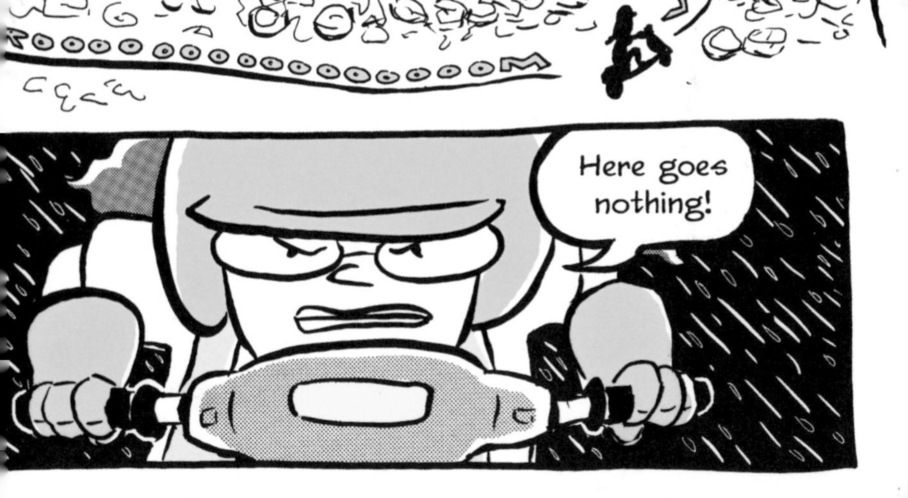
Here goes nothing!

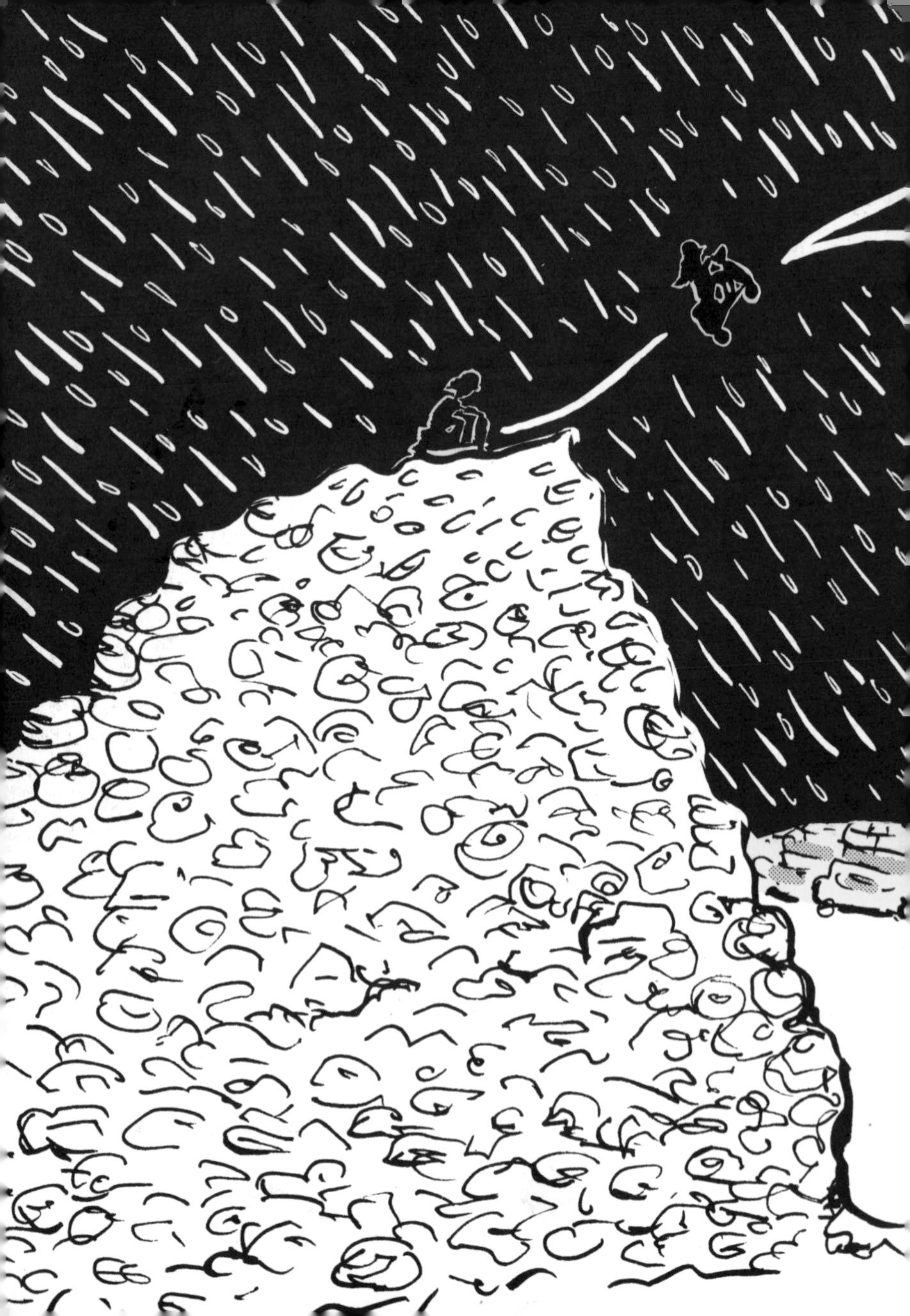

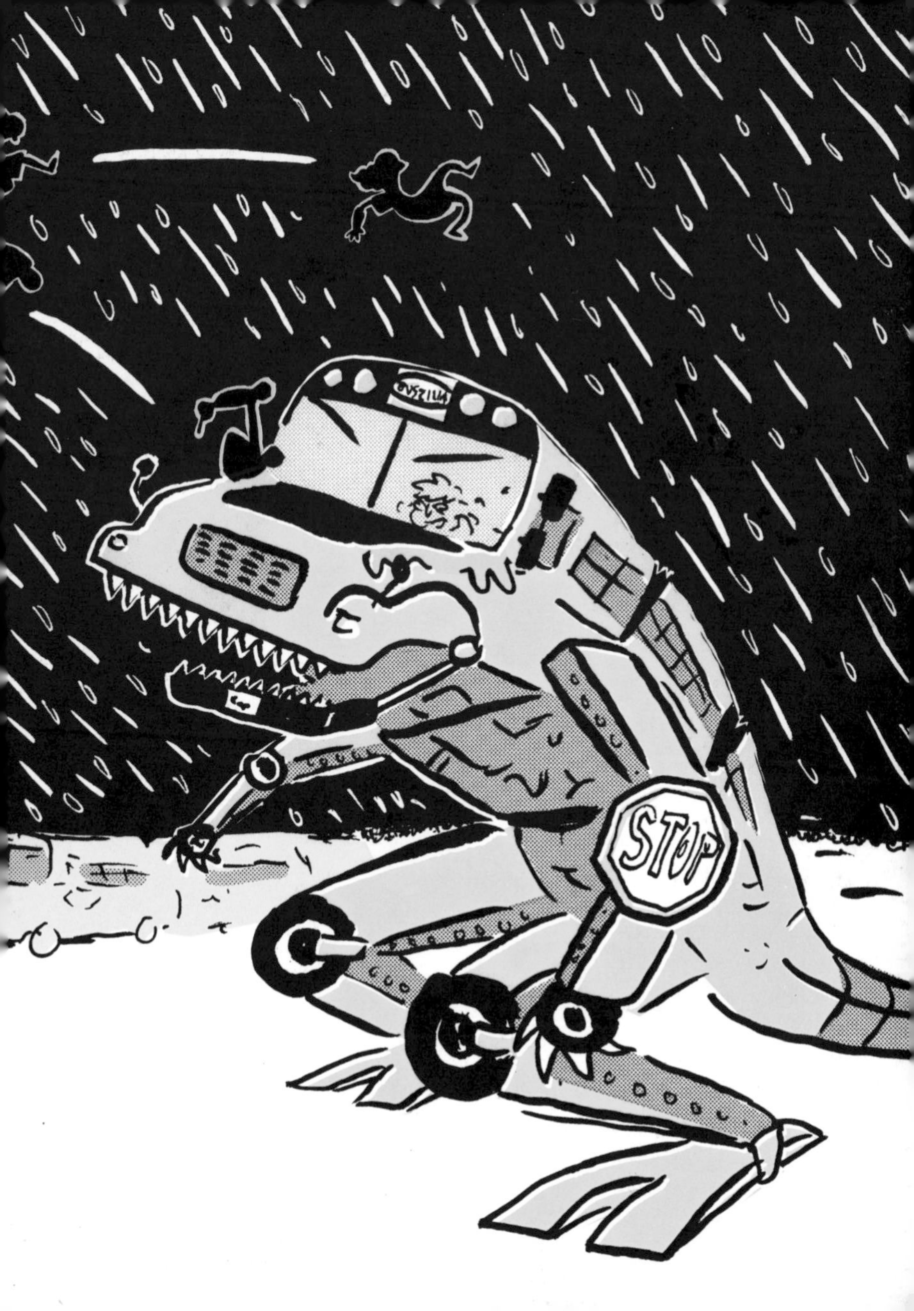
STOP

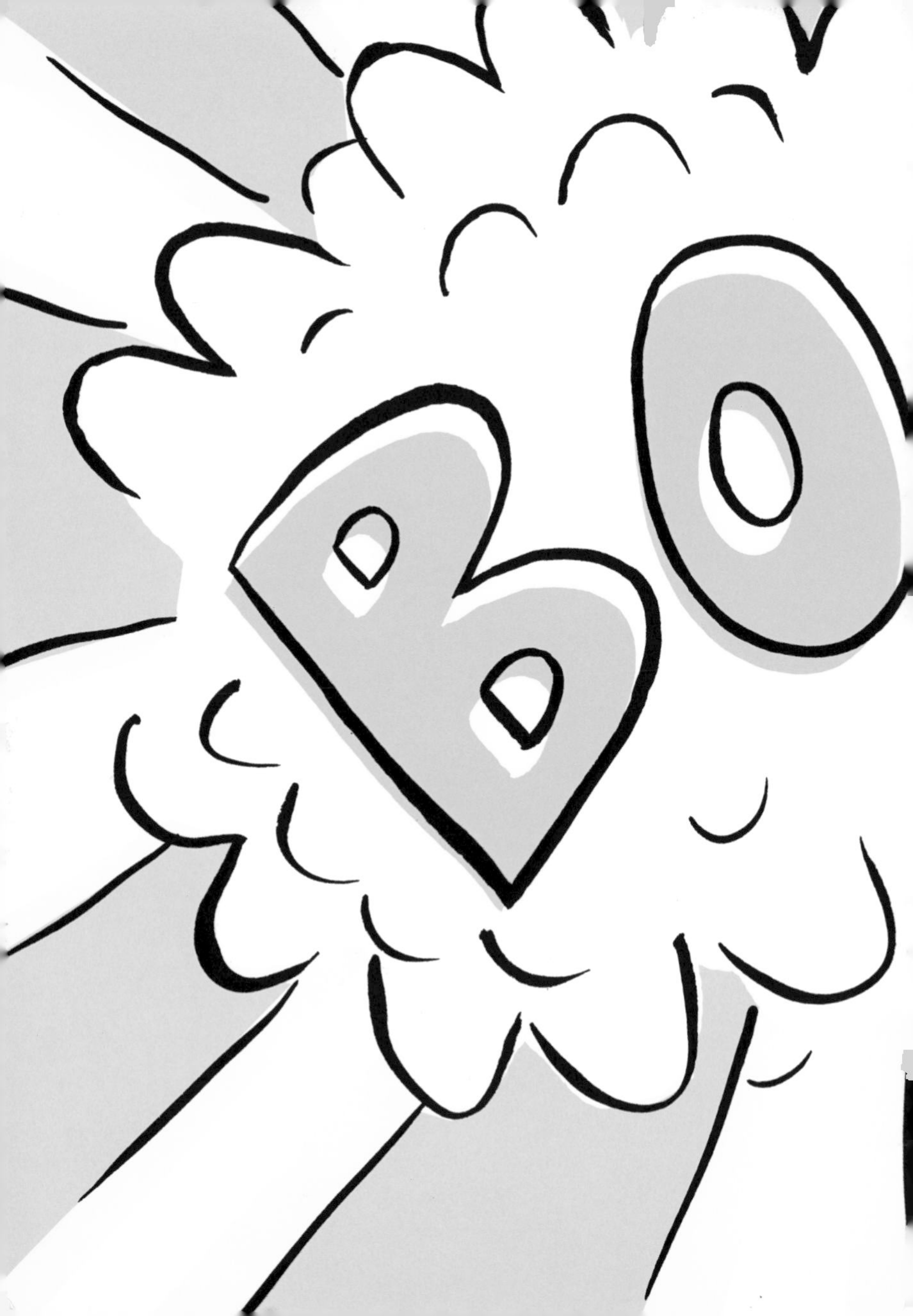
BO

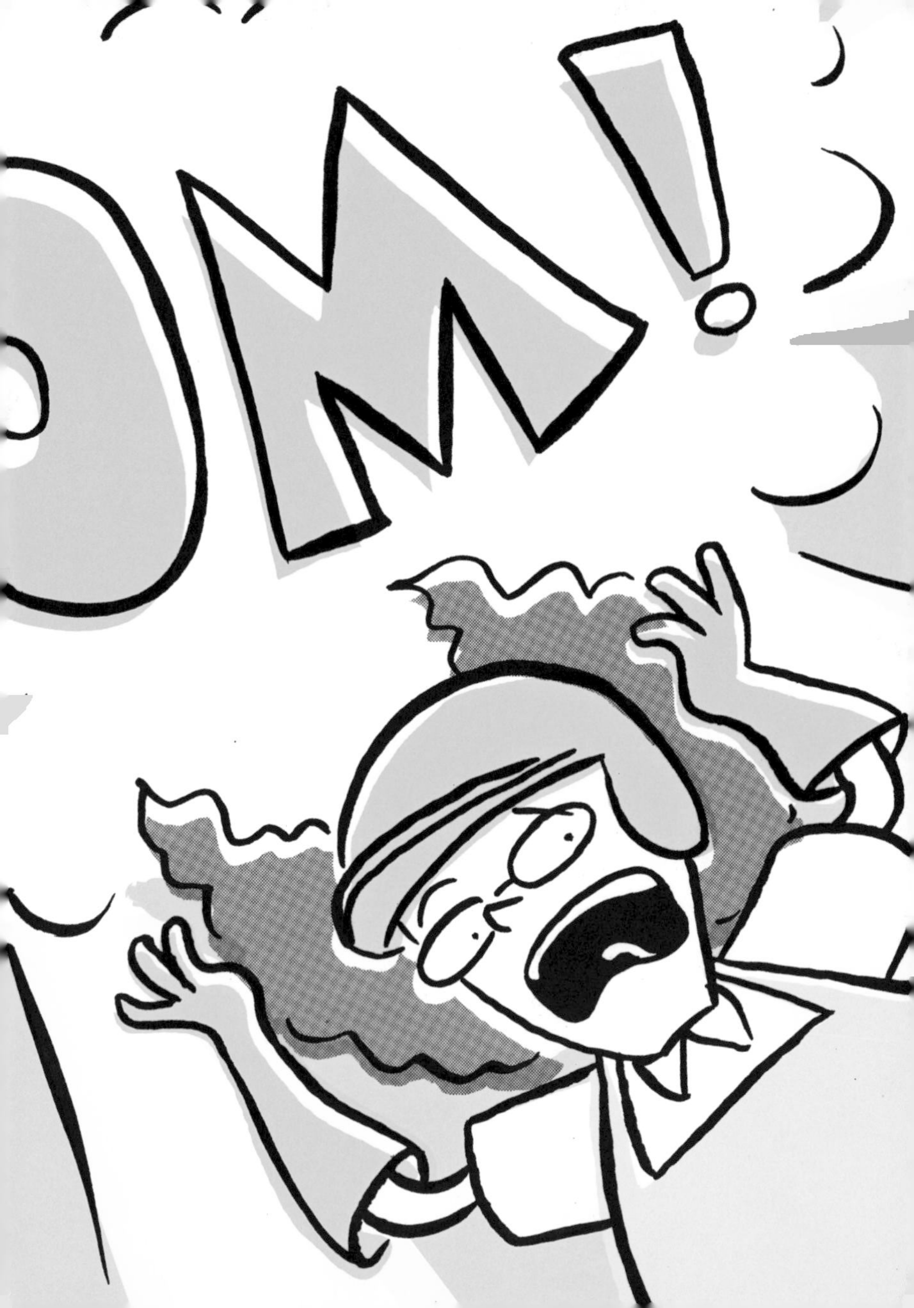
OM!

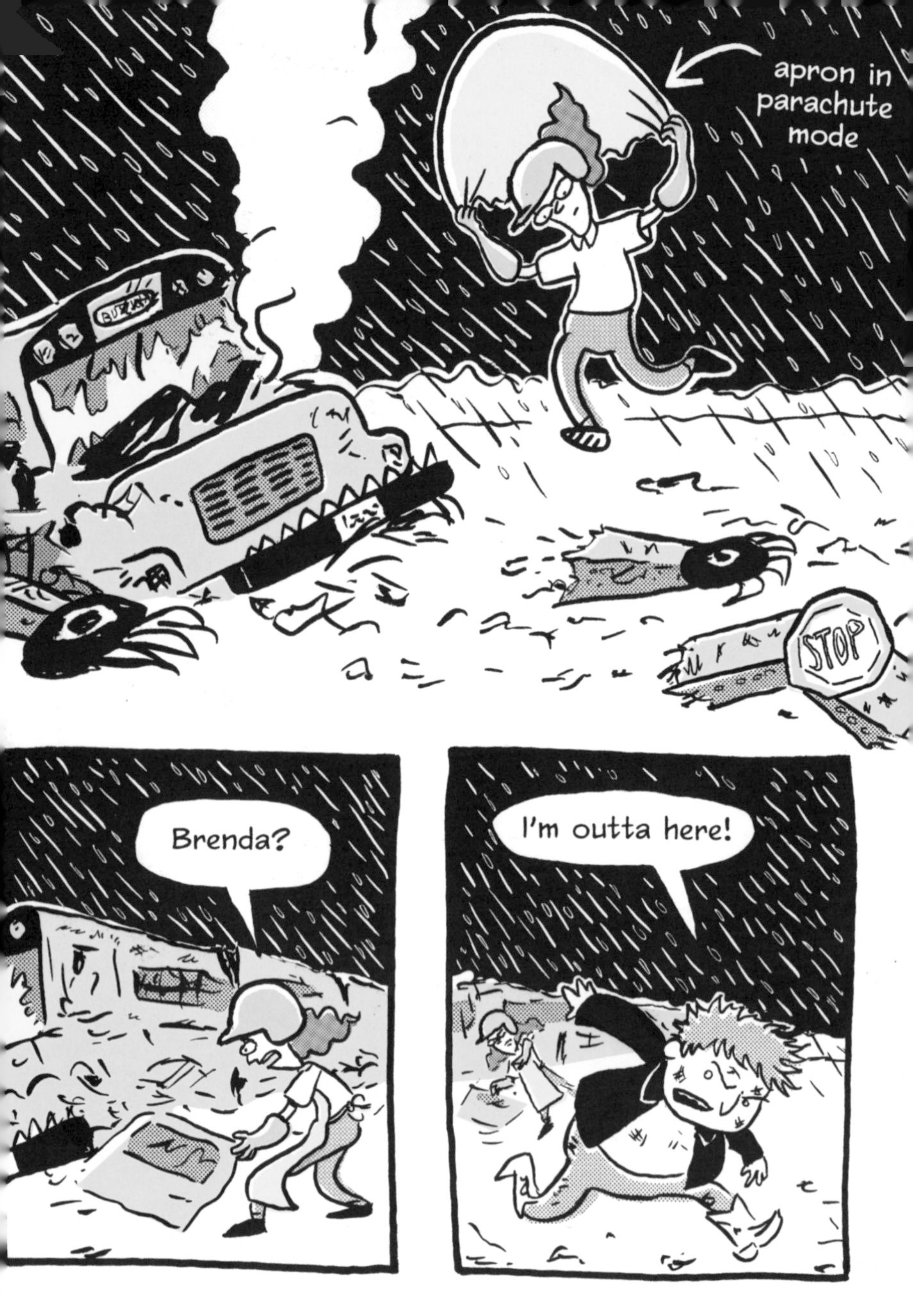
apron in parachute mode
STOP
Brenda?
I'm outta here!

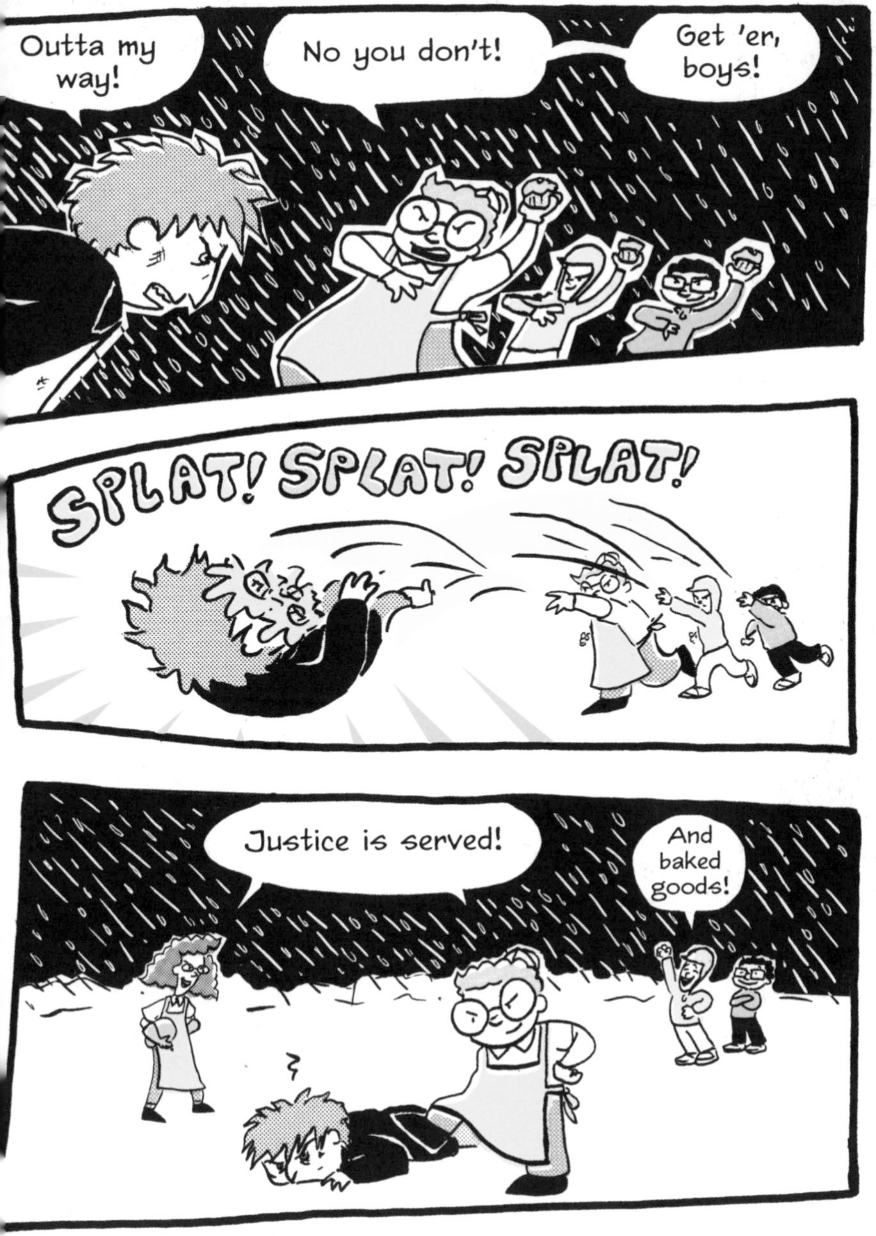
Outta my way!
No you don't!
Get 'er, boys!
SPLAT! SPLAT! SPLAT!
Justice is served!
And baked goods!

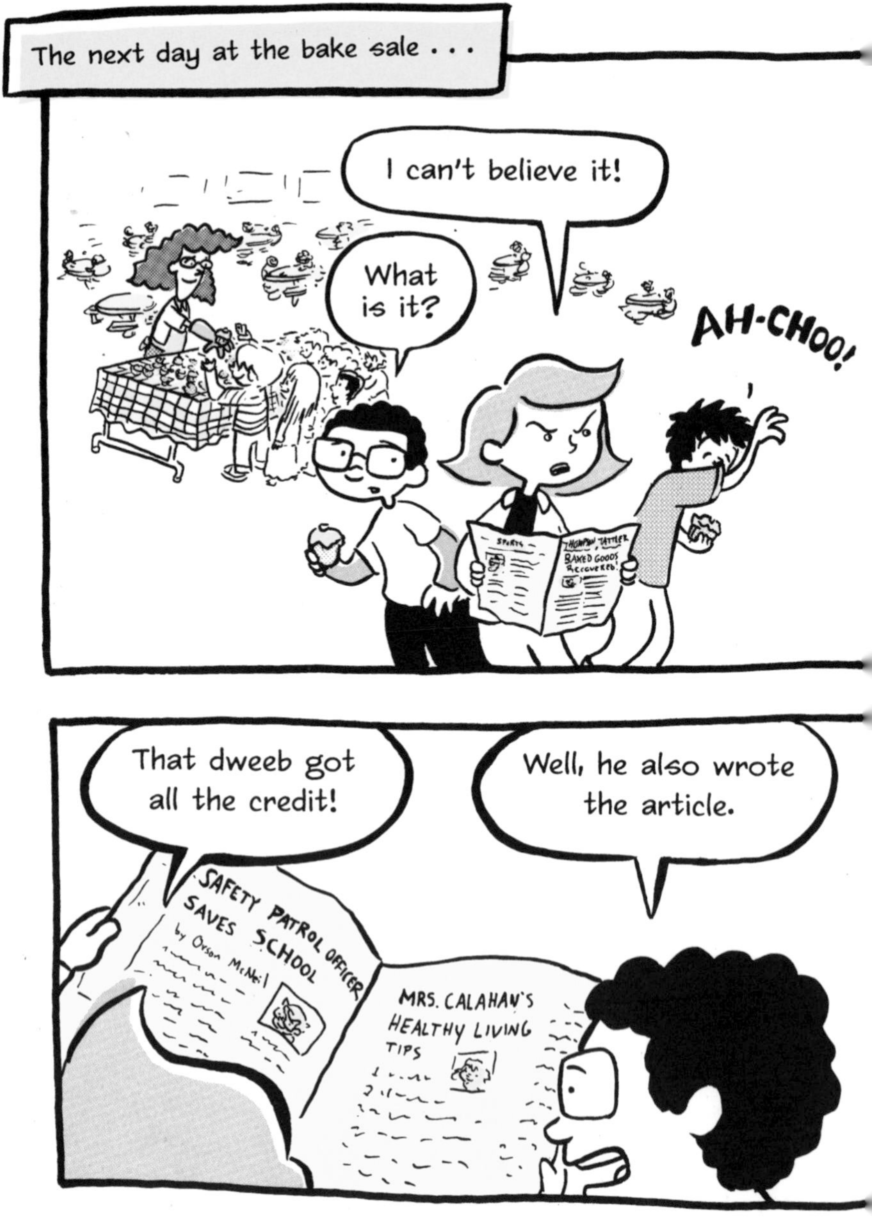
The next day at the bake sale . . .
I can't believe it!
What is it?
AH-CHOO!
BAKED GOODS RECOVERED!
That dweeb got all the credit!
Well, he also wrote the article.
SAFETY PATROL OFFICER SAVES SCHOOL
by Orson McNeil
MRS. CALAHAN'S HEALTHY LIVING TIPS

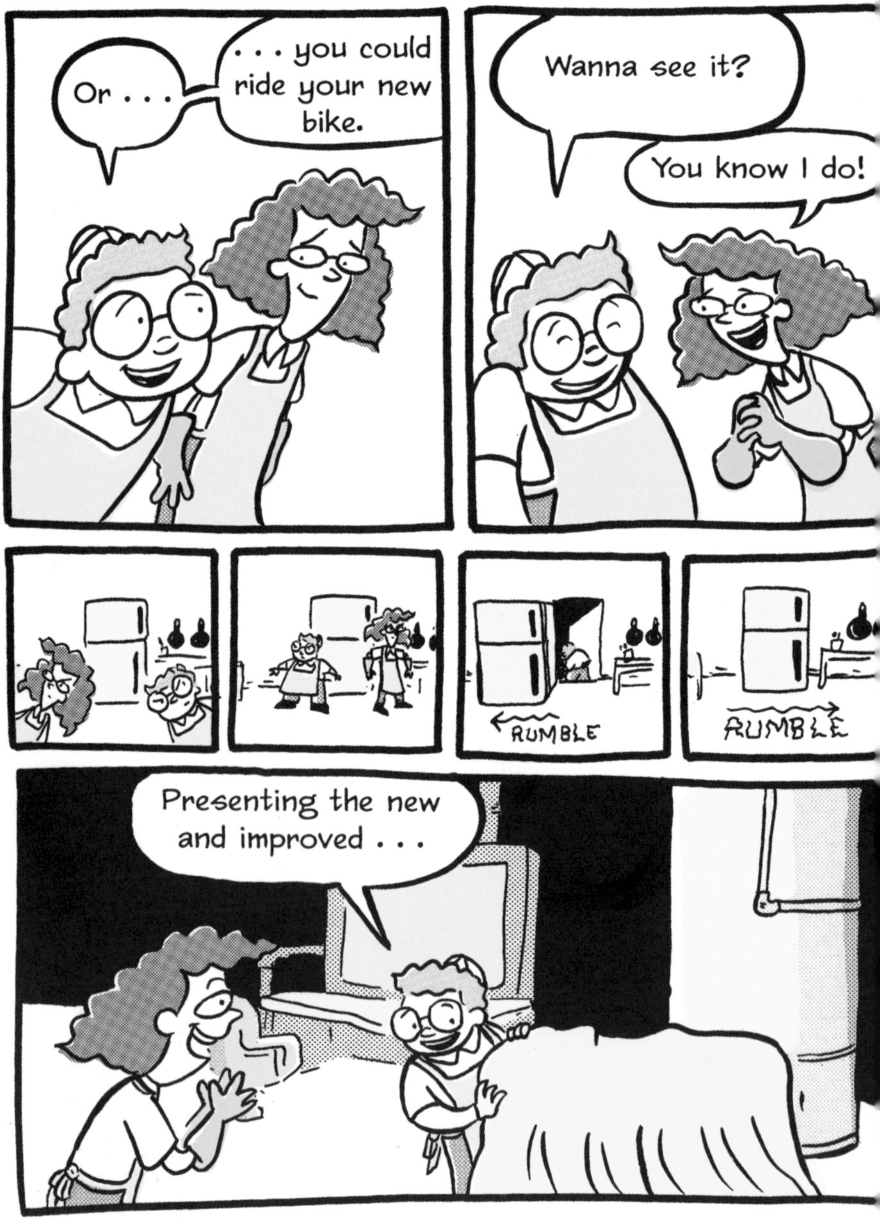
Or . . .
. . . you could ride your new bike.
Wanna see it?
You know I do!
RUMBLE
RUMBLE
Presenting the new and improved . . .

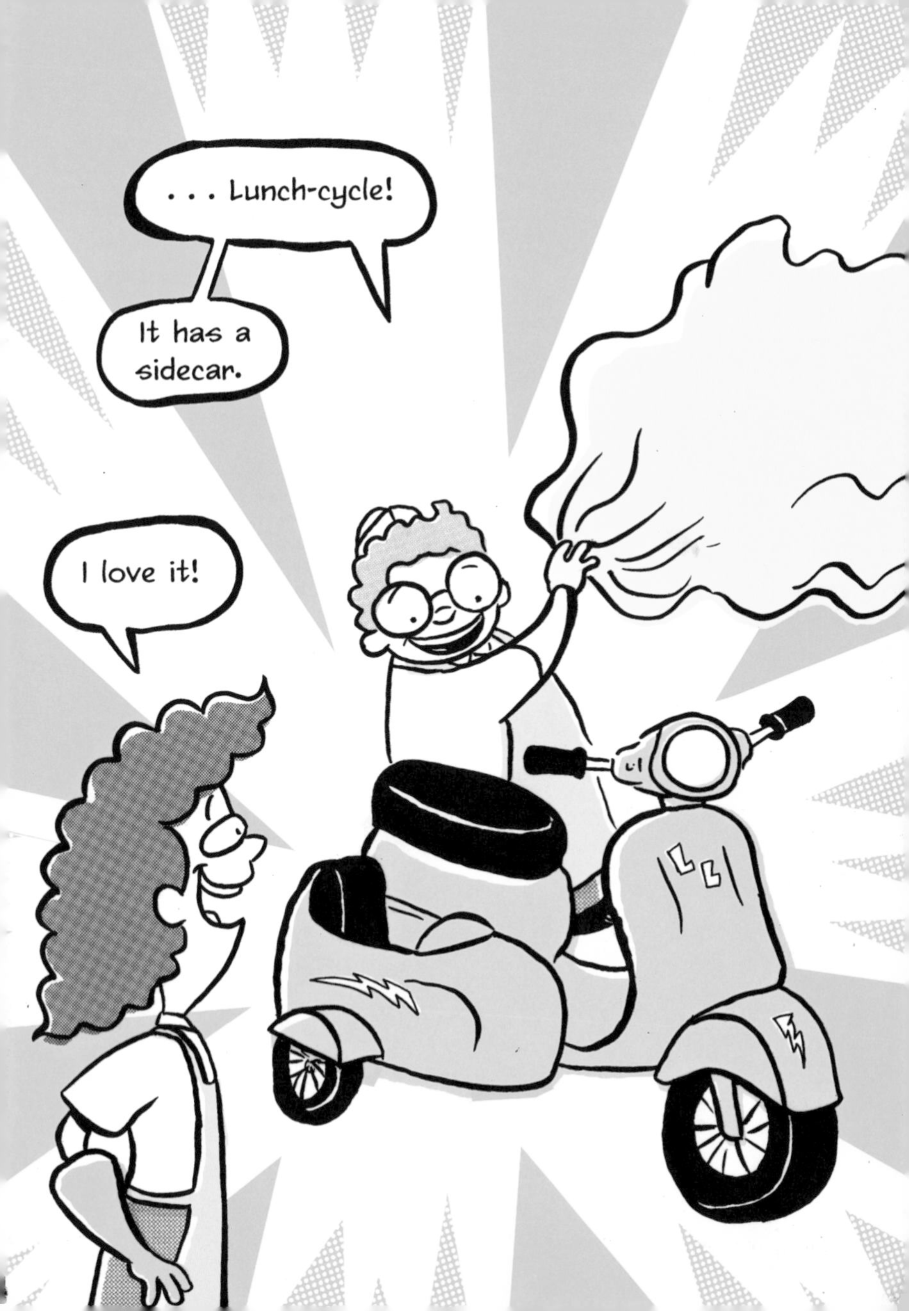

. . . Lunch-cycle!
It has a sidecar.
I love it!

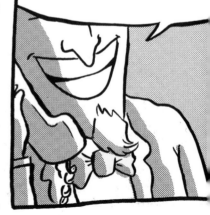

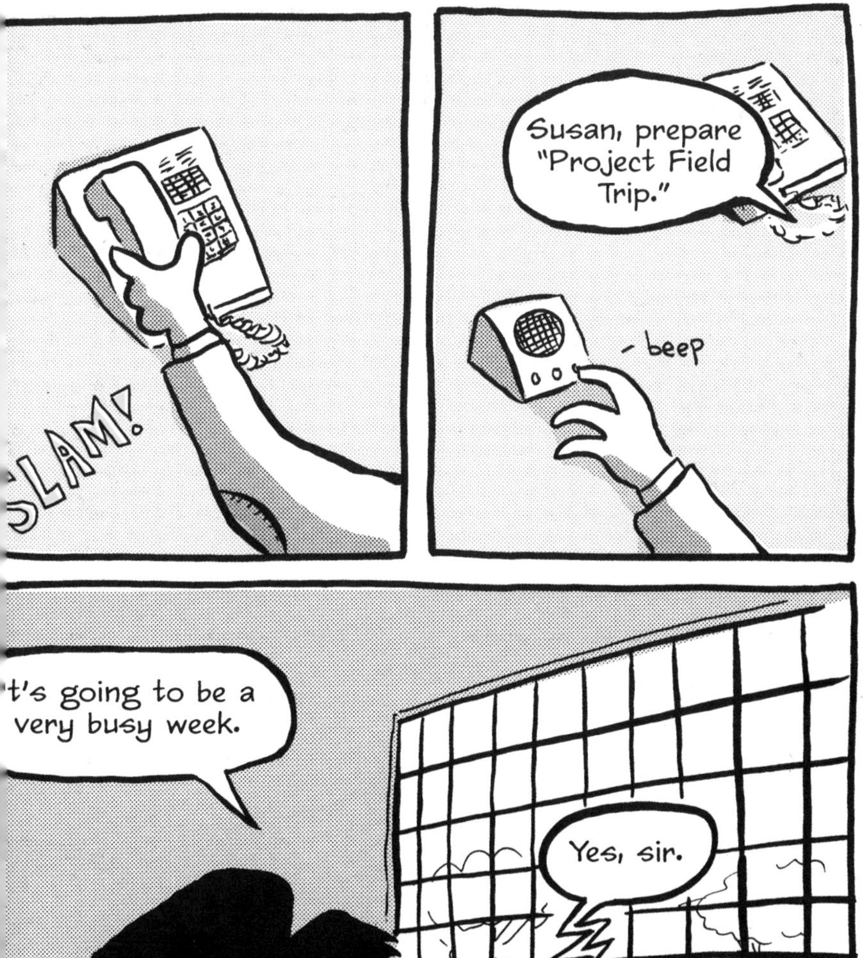
SLAM!
Susan, prepare "Project Field Trip."
- beep
't's going to be a very busy week.
Yes, sir.

FOR RICH AND DAWN
–J.J.K.

The author would like to acknowledge the color assist in this book by Joey Weiser.

THIS IS A BORZOI BOOK PUBLISHED BY ALFRED A. KNOPF

All rights reserved. Published in the United States by Alfred A. Knopf, an imprint of Random House Children's Books, a division of Random House, Inc., New York.

Knopf, Borzoi Books, and the colophon are registered trademarks of Random House, Inc.

Visit us on the Web! www.randomhouse.com/kids

Educators and librarians, for a variety of teaching tools,
visit us at www.randomhouse.com/teachers

Library of Congress Cataloging-in-Publication Data
Krosoczka, Jarrett J.
Lunch Lady and the bake sale bandit / Jarrett J. Krosoczka. — 1st ed.
p. cm.
Summary: Lunch Lady, Betty, and the Breakfast Bunch must figure out who is stealing the good from the bake sale.
ISBN 978-0-375-86729-3 (trade pbk.) — ISBN 978-0-375-96729-0 (lib. bdg.)
1. Graphic novels. [1. Graphic novels. 2. School lunchrooms, cafeterias, etc.—Fiction.
3. Stealing—Fiction. 4. Schools—Fiction. 5. Mystery and detective stories.] I. Title.
PZ7.7.K76Ltm 2010
[Fic]—dc22
2010012781

The text of this book is set in Hedge Backwards.
The illustrations in this book were created using ink on paper and digital coloring.

MANUFACTURED IN MALAYSIA
December 2010
10 9 8 7

First Edition